The F

GORDON SNELL

POOLBEG

Published 1997 by
Poolbeg Press Ltd,
123 Baldoyle Industrial Estate,
Dublin 13, Ireland

© Gordon Snell 1997

The moral right of the author has been asserted.

The Publishers gratefully acknowledge the support of
The Arts Council.

A catalogue record for this book is available from the
British Library.

ISBN 1 85371 797 5

Illustration by Peter Hanan
Cover design by Poolbeg Group Services Ltd
Set by Poolbeg Group Services Ltd in Stone 9.5/14
Printed and bound in Great Britain by
Cox & Wyman Ltd, Reading, Berks.

For dearest Maeve, with all my love

CHAPTER ONE

Grandpa

"Get ready now," said Dessy.

Brendan and Molly stood side by side, their hands pawing the air. They were pretending to be horses ready to race.

Dessy called out, "On your marks!"

"You don't say 'on your marks' in a horse-race," said Molly. "That's athletics."

"Listen to the jockey talking!" said Dessy. "I tell you, I wouldn't bet on *you*."

"At least I can ride a horse," Molly answered back. "And that's more than you can say for *some* of the people round here." She stared pointedly at Dessy.

Brendan said, "Listen, are we going to have a horse-race, or a fight on the track?"

"OK," said Dessy, "line up then, and stop slagging the starter. Don't forget, I've got the gun." He held up a paper bag. Then he blew into it so that it swelled with air, and clapped his hands on it.

It made a satisfying pop.

Brendan and Molly, hands still pawing the air, began to run around the small scrappy park at the end of the road where Brendan lived. Dessy lived just around the corner and Brendan's cousin Molly and her mother were up from the country staying with Brendan's family in Dublin. It wasn't a holiday this time, but what Brendan's parents called a Family Conference, about Brendan and Molly's grandfather and where he should live.

As the other two kept running, Dessy began to call out like a racing commentator. "They're away from the start now, and just coming to the first fence, and Molly Malone has stumbled – no, she's up again, but it looks like Brendan the Navigator is well in the lead, though he's carrying a lot of weight, in fact he's fat as a pig! Will he make it over the jump? Yes, he has, though he's feeling the pace and panting like a wart-hog – and Molly Malone is wheeling her barrow and spilling cockles and mussels all over the show. Up they go again, and it's neck and neck as they reach the last lap, and the crowd roars, and they're coming down the final straight – it could be a photo-finish except their faces might break the camera . . . and it's all over!"

Molly and Brendan stood side by side, breathing heavily.

"Well, who won?" asked Brendan, between gasps.

"Let me see," said Dessy, pretending to examine a photograph.

Then he said, "Nobody. It's a dead heat. The starter gets the prize." He produced a chocolate bar.

"Like heck he does!" said Brendan, snatching at the bar.

Dessy held it away from him, but Molly came round the other side and seized it.

"The winner!" she shouted. She began to run, but the other two grabbed hold of her, and soon all three of them were wrestling on the ground.

Brendan called out, "Time!" and they stopped and sat up.

Molly said, "Where's the prize? I'll let you share it."

They looked around. The chocolate bar was on the ground, squashed flat.

They went and sat on a park bench, and shared out the flattened chocolate.

"Grandpa Locky knows all about racing," said Brendan.

"Yes, he's an expert," said Molly.

"Too much of an expert, according to my father," said Brendan. "He says Grandpa will lose all his money on the horses one day. But Grandpa just laughs. You see, most of the time he comes out winning. And that seems to annoy my father even more."

"My grandma doesn't care about horses," said Dessy. "She likes the Lottery – but she never wins. My mother is always going on at her about the money she wastes."

"Maybe all parents go on at their own parents," said Molly.

"Just like they do at their own children," said Brendan.

They all nodded, thinking about the strange ways of parents.

Grandparents were easier to get on with. They

seemed more relaxed and interested and happy to let you do what you liked.

"What is it you call your grandfather? Locky?" Dessy said. "What kind of a name is that? Does he pick locks, or what?"

"Of course not, you eejit," said Brendan. "It's just sort of a nickname."

"It's short for Loughlin," said Molly. "We've called him Grandpa Locky as long as I can remember."

"So have we," said Brendan. "You see, he's my mother's father, as well as Molly's mother's."

"He's lovely," said Molly, "always telling us jokes and stories and taking us to see places."

"Hey, maybe I could tell him some of *my* jokes," said Dessy. "What does a cat say when you tread on its tail?"

"Dunno," said Molly and Brendan wearily.

"Meee-OUCH!" Dessy roared with laughter. "Do you think he'll like it?"

"You can try it out, if he comes to live with us," said Brendan.

"I hope he'll come and live with *us*," said Molly. "My parents want him to."

"So do mine," said Brendan.

"Where does he live now?" asked Dessy.

"On his own, in a house in the next town from us," said Molly. "He seems fine to me, but our parents say he can't manage by himself any longer. They're always going on about it."

They were going on about it at tea, later that day.

"He's a stubborn old man, that's what he is," said Brendan's mother.

"Too used to having his own way," said Molly's mother.

"That's because after your own mother died, you all spoiled him rotten," said Mr O'Hara, Brendan's father.

"We did not!"

"You should have suggested he moved out of that house long ago, it's much bigger than he needs."

"But it's his home," said Molly's mother.

"Yes, and if you're not careful, he'll burn it down or something. Remember how he set that towel alight, trying to dry it too close to the fire? And the time he left the bath tap running and nearly flooded the place?"

"We all agree he can't go on living there on his own," said Brendan's mother.

"Why can't he come here?" asked Brendan.

"Or to live with us in Ballygandon?" said Molly.

"You know we've asked him to, but he just won't hear of it," said her mother. "He says he doesn't want to be a bother to us."

"He's more of a bother staying where he is," said Brendan's father.

"Well, that's why we're here, to work out what to do," said Molly's mother.

Brendan thought the Family Conference wasn't getting very far. The arguments just seemed to go round in circles.

The telephone rang. When Brendan's father came back from answering it, he said, "We might as well suspend the Family Conference for the moment. The subject of it is arriving tomorrow."

"What do you mean?" asked Mrs O'Hara.

"That was Locky on the phone. He says we're to stop worrying. He's solved the problem, and he won't be living on his own any more. He's getting the train up here tomorrow to tell us all about it."

This news caused even more argument than there had been before. What did Locky mean? Was someone else coming to live with him? Was he going to live with some friend locally? Had he got a room in the town?

Molly said, "Perhaps he's getting married again."

"WHAT?!" her mother exclaimed. They all gazed at Molly, shocked into silence. Then the conversation became even more heated. Molly wished she'd kept her mouth shut. She made a sign to Brendan, and they went quietly out of the room, leaving their parents arguing.

The next day was a Saturday. Brendan's father went to meet Grandpa Locky from the train, and Molly and Brendan went with him.

They stood on the platform among the crowds of people hurrying to and fro or standing about waiting. The train drew in, and doors began to open even before it had stopped. They waited.

Finally Brendan shouted, "There he is!"

Locky was a tall man, with curly grey hair, topped by a jaunty green hat that had a tiny feather in the hat-band. He was wearing an old-fashioned but smart dark grey suit, and a jazzy red tie. He liked wearing bright ties, he said they cheered people up, though Brendan's mother said you'd need sun-glasses to look at them.

He was carrying a tote-bag with CHICAGO WHITE SOX printed on it, a souvenir of a visit to a baseball game on a long-ago trip to the USA.

Brendan and Molly rushed forward to greet him calling, "Grandpa Locky! Grandpa Locky!"

"Well, hello there!" their grandfather called back. He had a booming voice that could almost be heard all over the station.

He bent down to give Molly a kiss, and shook Brendan by the hand. Brendan's father came over to them.

"Hello, Locky," he said. "Welcome to Dublin."

"Good to see you, Pat," said Locky. "How's the newspaper game? You must give me the lowdown on the latest scandals."

"No shortage of those," said Brendan's father. "But it's *your* news we want to hear."

"All in good time," said Locky. "Meanwhile, help yourselves to these." He produced two bags of toffees and handed them to Brendan and Molly. "Good for the teeth," he said, and winked.

When they got home, his two daughters were bombarding him with questions almost as soon as he got in the door. What was all the mystery? What was he planning? Had he done anything silly?

"Hold on, hold on," said Locky. "Settle me down with a drink in my hand, and I will tell all."

They sat round the dining table. Locky had insisted that Brendan and Molly should be there too. He took a sip of his beer, and looked round at them all.

"Come on, Dad," said Brendan's mother sharply. "Stop making a drama out of it. Just tell us."

"I've found the answer," said Locky, smiling. "Horseshoe House."

"Horseshoe House?" asked Molly's mother. "Is this something to do with your racing friends?"

"Not at all," said Locky. "It's the name of a big house. A residential home, they call it. It's out in the country, about half way between Dublin and Ballygandon. Easy for visiting, so you can both keep an eye on me."

"But what do you know about it?"

"Have you seen it?"

"What will it cost?"

The questions came rattling out like some hectic quiz show.

"Everything is taken care of," said Locky calmly. "I visited a friend of mine there a couple of years ago before he moved abroad. It's a grand place, and the woman who runs it is very kind and efficient. A widow, called Mrs Boyd. She only has half a dozen or so people there, and provides everything. Your own room and all meals."

"It sounds expensive," said Brendan's father.

"Good value, I'd say," Locky said. "I've got enough saved to pay for it for a while, and then when I've sold the house there'll be no problem. Besides, who knows, I might have a big win on the horses!" He smiled happily. The others did not.

"Well, when can we have a look at it?" said Brendan's mother.

"When I move in, if you like," said Locky. "I've arranged to go in next week."

"You mean it's all fixed already?" Molly's mother was astonished, and not very pleased.

"Why didn't you ask us to check it out?" said Brendan's mother.

"I didn't want to bother you," said his grandfather. "Besides, you kept saying I couldn't live on my own any more. Now you won't have to worry."

Later when Brendan and Molly told Dessy about it as they sat on the park bench between games of football, they confessed they were puzzled. Grandpa Locky seemed to have done all that their parents wanted – yet after he told them, they got quite annoyed with him. They thought he should have checked everything with them first.

They fussed about what he was up to as much as they did about the activities of Brendan or Molly.

Dessy said, "The answer is he should tell them as little as possible. That's my way of getting on at home. What they don't know can't bother them. He should have moved in, and *then* told them."

"Maybe you're right," said Brendan. "Anyway, he's fixed it all up, so there isn't much anyone can do about it."

"Except go in with him on the day, and make sure everything's all right," said Molly. "And our mothers are certainly going to do that."

"And we're going with them!" said Brendan.

CHAPTER TWO

Horseshoe House

Brendan and Dessy were standing by the gate of Brendan's house.

His mother was going to drive with him down to meet Molly and her mother at Locky's. Then they would all bring him to his new place, Horseshoe House.

"Your grandfather's lucky," said Dessy. "Imagine being able to choose where you live, instead of being stuck at home like the rest of us."

"Home's all right," said Brendan. "Anyway, where do you want to live?"

"Some place with a television in each room, and my own football pitch," said Dessy. "And a kitchen staff to serve me hamburgers and chips whenever I want them."

"Why not move into the President's place up in Phoenix Park? That would suit you, I reckon."

"Perfect!" said Dessy. "I'll stand for election, next time around."

"In the meantime," said Brendan, "I'll check out Grandpa Locky's new place. Maybe they'd have room for you."

"You'd have to be ancient to go in there, wouldn't you?"

"Well, we could do an Oisín job on you. Remember how he left Tír na nÓg and turned into an old man as soon as he touched the ground?"

"I'd rather stay at home, thanks."

"Anyway," said Brendan, "Grandpa's new place doesn't sound too bad. There's even some kind of ghost there, he says. A Phantom Horseman. That's why it's called Horseshoe House."

"A Phantom Horseman, eh? A bit tricky when it comes to a photo finish."

"Brendan, stop loafing around there, and give us a hand." It was his father, coming out of the front door with a suitcase and a cardboard box. Brendan went and took the box from him. It had towels and a rug in it.

"Your mother seems to want to furnish the place, as far as I can see," said Brendan's father, as they put the things into the car.

"I want to make sure Dad's got everything he needs," said Brendan's mother, joining them.

"Well, he should have, for the price they're charging."

"It's worth it if he's happy there," said Brendan's mother. "Right, we're off. In you get, Brendan."

"See you, Dessy," said Brendan.

"See you," said Dessy, "and if you meet the Phantom Horseman, put a fiver on him for me."

Molly and her mother were waiting to meet them at Grandpa Locky's. Molly's mother seemed agitated.

"What's the matter?" asked her sister.

"Wait till I tell you – there have been changes at this Horseshoe place, and Dad didn't even think to let us know."

"It's no problem," said Locky. "Stop fussing, Maureen."

"What's this all about?" asked Brendan's mother.

"It's nothing to worry over," said Locky.

"Nothing?" exclaimed Mrs Donovan. "Just that there are new people running Horseshoe House since Dad agreed to go in. Mrs Boyd has swanned off to California, would you believe?"

"She hasn't 'swanned off'," said Locky, "her daughter needs her, so she's gone to be with her. Her nephew and his wife have taken over Horseshoe House, that's all."

"We'll need to know just what the set-up is before we take him there," said Brendan's mother. "We'll ring them straight away."

They went to the room where the telephone was and shut the door. Locky grinned at Brendan and Molly.

"Now, while they're sorting that out," said Locky, "maybe you'll give me a hand with my packing?"

They went into a room which Locky called his Den. It had a lot of books on shelves, and a desk, and chairs with papers and magazines scattered on them.

"I'll move some of this lot into the new place when I see how much room I've got," he said. "But there are some things I want to make sure I take." He put an empty hold-all on to the desk.

12

"Now, could you hand me that pile of papers and stuff?"

Brendan and Molly brought papers and magazines over to Locky and he quickly chose the ones he wanted to take, and put them in the hold-all. They were mostly racing papers and books on horses and guides to form.

"Your mothers don't think I'll need all this," said Locky, "but I like to keep up with the racing scene."

"I wonder if you'll see the Phantom Horseman, Grandpa," said Molly.

"You never know," said Locky. "Maybe I'll even find the missing horseshoe."

"What horseshoe, Grandpa?" asked Brendan.

Locky crammed a final batch of papers into the hold-all and zipped it up. Then he sat down on the desk, his long legs stretched out.

"It's a tragic story," he said. "They say that a couple of hundred years ago, there was a young man called Daniel who was in love with a local girl called Aoife. But the son of the Lord who lived in the big house took a fancy to her, and came and snatched her away. Daniel decided to rescue her."

"What did he do?" asked Brendan.

"One night he got on a horse and rode towards the house, but he had to keep off the roads in case he was spotted. So he rode through the woods on the estate. There's an old stone burial vault with a monument there, belonging to the family. He came to it unexpectedly and tried to jump over it. But a horseshoe came off, and the horse fell. Daniel was thrown off and killed."

"So it's *his* ghost that is the Phantom Horseman?" asked Molly.

"That's right. He and his horse are always trying to jump the stone monument. But the legend says they will never succeed until the horseshoe is found. Then the haunting will stop. And until then, there's a threat of doom hanging over the whole place, including Horseshoe House."

"Maybe you shouldn't go to live there, Grandpa," said Molly.

"Oh, I'm not scared of ghosts and threats of doom," said Locky. "Besides, I'm old – I don't suppose the disaster will strike till after my time."

"Perhaps the horseshoe will be found," said Brendan. "Hey, I've got an idea. Why don't Molly and I go and search for it, whenever we come and visit you?"

"Good thinking," said Locky.

"We could bring Dessy too," said Molly. "The Ballygandon Gang's Private Eyes can surely track down a lost horseshoe!"

Locky smiled. "I'm sure you'll have the case cracked in no time."

"Oh, there you are!" said Brendan's mother, looking in at the door. "Well, we've talked to the Boyds, and they certainly sound pleasant enough. They said they'd show us round and tell us everything when we get there."

"You see," said Locky. "No problem."

A driveway lined with big dark-leaved bushes

wound its way up to Horseshoe House. It came out in front of a large house made of old red brick with stone-framed windows. At the front was a big stone porch with a coat of arms carved on top of it.

They parked the car nearby and all five of them got out and gathered in the porch. They looked around for a bell or a door-knocker, but couldn't see one.

"How about this?" said Brendan. There was a metal ring hanging from a chain in the porch ceiling. He pulled it. From inside there was the clang of a bell.

The big oak door opened with a creaking sound. A girl of about eighteen, with short fair hair and wearing a pink uniform rather like a nurse's, stood there, smiling.

"Hello there," she said. "You must be the Ryan family."

"Yes, I'm Loughlin Ryan," said Locky.

"And we're his daughters," said Brendan's mother, stepping forward. "We spoke to Mr and Mrs Boyd on the phone."

"And these are my grandchildren," said Locky. "I hope you've got room for us all?"

"Well . . ." the girl looked alarmed.

"Don't worry, I was only joking," said Locky, ignoring the disapproving expressions of his daughters. "I'm the only one who's planning to stay."

The girl looked relieved. "Please come in. My name is Carrie. I'm one of the Carers here. If you'd just wait in here, I'll tell Mr and Mrs Boyd you've arrived."

She showed them into a room off the hall. It had chairs around the side and a table in the middle with a vase of flowers, and magazines and papers on it.

"It looks like a doctor's waiting room," said Brendan's mother.

Soon Mr and Mrs Boyd came in. They introduced themselves as Gerry and Maura, and asked everyone to sit down. Gerry Boyd was a plump, cheery-looking man in a brown tweed suit. He had fair wispy hair which was long and untidy. His wife Maura was dressed in a smart green suit, with a creamy blouse and a glittery brooch on the lapel. Her hair looked carefully groomed in elaborate copper-coloured waves, and she wore a lot of make-up.

"Sorry if all this seems a bit sudden, our taking over," said Gerry Boyd. "My aunt's only got the one daughter, my cousin Helen, and she's not well. Of course she had to go over to California to help out."

"How long will she be away?" asked Molly's mother.

"Hard to say, at this stage," said Maura. "But she's put us in full charge here. We're looking forward to getting the place into shape."

"What's wrong with it?" Brendan's mother was suspicious.

Gerry Boyd smiled and said hastily, "What Maura means is that we want to make a few improvements and add a few more luxuries to make life even more comfortable than it is already. Our guests are perfectly happy, I assure you. Some of them have been here for years."

"I'm sure you will like it here, Mr Ryan," said Maura Boyd with a brassy kind of smile.

"Perhaps we could look around . . ." said Brendan's mother.

"Of course, of course, come with us," said Gerry Boyd.

"The children won't be interested, I'm sure," said his wife. "Why don't you both wait for us here?"

There seemed to be no choice. The others went out of the room, and Brendan and Molly started to look through the magazines on the table. But they were all about gardens and furniture and country life.

They looked out of the window which was at the side of the house. There was a bit of garden with some shrubs, and a small statue. Beyond that they could see the trees of a dense wood.

"Those must be the woods the Phantom Horseman rides through," said Brendan.

"I wonder where the monument is," said Molly.

Brendan walked over to the door. "There's only one way to find out," he said.

CHAPTER THREE

Strange Voices

Brendan opened the door quietly. They peered out into the hallway. No one seemed to be about.

They tiptoed across to the big front door. Brendan took hold of the brass handle and turned it. He pulled the door. There was a loud creak as it slowly opened. They looked around, but no one came, so they slipped out, closing the door behind them.

They went round to the side of the house, and found the garden and the statue they had seen from the window. Then they went through the shrubs and into the wood.

Under the trees there was a thick growth of tangled bushes and brambles, but they picked up sticks and managed to beat a pathway through. They came to an area full of tall fir-trees, and here the ground was clearer. Brendan could imagine Daniel on his horse, weaving his way between the trees, on his rescue mission.

They came to a pond with rushes around it. "I wonder if he jumped over that?" said Brendan.

"It doesn't look very deep," said Molly. "A horse could probably wade through it."

"Can ghosts get wet?" Brendan wondered.

"If we see the Phantom Horseman, perhaps we'll find out," said Molly.

"I don't suppose he'll turn up in the day-time." Brendan stopped and leaned against a tree. Suddenly he said, "Hey, what's that?"

"What's what?" asked Molly.

"I thought I heard the sound of a horse's hooves."

They stood listening. Sure enough, there was a faint, regular drumming sound in the air.

"Where is it coming from?" Molly listened.

"I don't know," said Brendan. "It sounds quite near."

"Yes, it's close to us." Molly looked around. Then she grabbed Brendan's arm, and said sharply, "I'll throttle you one day, Brendan O'Hara! It was *you*, tapping on the back of the tree."

Brendan laughed. "I had you fooled there!" Then he gave a screech as Molly twisted his arm behind his back.

"OK, OK, I give in," he cried.

"I've a good mind to push you into that pond," said Molly. "Then you can tell me if you find any wet ghosts in there."

But she let go of his arm and said, "Come on, stop messing and we'll try and find that monument."

They moved on through the trees and came to a clump of dark shrubs. They pushed their way through and found themselves in a clearing. In the middle of it stood a large square structure, three times their own height, with stone steps all around it. Round the top of it were stone battlements, like the roof of a castle. There was thick green ivy growing over it, but here and there they could see slabs of marble underneath. "This is it!" Molly whispered.

"The monument," said Brendan. He wondered why he felt it necessary to whisper too. Surely they weren't afraid of waking someone buried inside?

But they both felt a weird stillness about the place, as though indeed something was asleep and could be roused at any moment. They remembered the story of the threat of doom that hung over the house. It would only be lifted, the story said, when the horseshoe was found. But finding it wasn't going to be easy.

They moved slowly towards the ivy-covered building. They went up the three levels of stone steps, which were covered with patches of moss and lichen. Molly reached out and put her hand on an area of grey marble.

"It's cold," she said, and shivered.

They made their way slowly around the Monument. At one point, there was a place that was free of ivy, where the marble had cracked. They could see a slit underneath. Brendan slid his fingers into it, then pushed his hand in.

"It feels quite crumbly inside," he said. "If we could pull the marble further apart, we could maybe dig our way in."

Molly was shocked. "We can't do that, it would be like disturbing a grave."

"I guess so," said Brendan. Then he pulled his hand out with a cry.

"What's up?" asked Molly.

"I felt something touch my hand." He looked at his hand in alarm.

"Get off, you're codding me again," said Molly.

"No, no – something touched me." Brendan had gone quite pale. They both stared at the slit. As they watched, a spider slid out of it, and scurried away into the ivy.

They both smiled, and Brendan looked very relieved. "Where do you think the horseshoe could be?" asked Molly.

"It could have got tangled up in the ivy, I suppose," Brendan said. "Or fallen on the ground and got buried, or even fallen through a crack into the inside . . ."

He peered into the slit in the wall of the monument. Then he frowned and looked worried.

"What's up?" asked Molly. Brendan put his finger to his lips, and then leaned towards the slit, putting his ear close to the opening.

"I'm sure I can hear something. A sort of a sighing sound."

"Let me listen." Molly put her ear to the opening and said, "Yes, I can hear it too. It's like some one saying eeee . . . eeee . . . eeee . . ."

"It must be the wind whistling in the crack," said Brendan.

"It sounds like a voice," Molly said. "Wait . . . What was the name of the girl the Phantom Horseman was in love with, the one he was trying to rescue?"

21

"Aoife, I think."

"Yes, that was it," said Brendan, "and that's what the sound is like. Someone crying the name Aoife, over and over again." They looked at each other in fright. Then they listened once more. The voice seemed to come from inside the monument, crying, "Aoife . . . Aoife . . . Aoife . . ."

"Perhaps they buried Daniel in there and his spirit is crying for his lost love," said Molly.

"You don't suppose it could be a real person, trapped in there?" asked Brendan in alarm.

"There's no way to get in," said Molly, "or if there is, it's been covered up with ivy and not disturbed for hundreds of years."

But they made their way around the monument, just in case they could see some sign of a doorway. There was none. They listened again at the slit, but now the crying voice seemed to have stopped.

Then Molly said, "Listen, I hear something else. It sounds like singing." Indeed, a deep voice could be heard not far away, singing the words of the operatic song, *Nessun Dorma*.

"That's the World Cup anthem they had in Italy," said Brendan. "At least that can't be a ghost!"

"It's coming from over there in the woods," said Molly. "Let's go and see."

"They moved into the trees. Peering round a bush, they saw a man in what looked like a loose white cloak, with a straw hat on his head. He was sitting on a stool, in front of a half-finished painting, which was fixed to the tripod. He had a board in one hand, with splatters of paint on it, and a brush in his other hand, with which he dabbed at the picture.

Brendan trod on a branch which gave a crack. The painter looked round and saw them. "Well, hello there!" he said.

Brendan and Molly stepped out from behind the bush, mumbling an awkward greeting. They felt as if they had been caught spying.

But the painter was friendly enough. "How do you do?" he said, taking off his hat in a mock gesture of politeness. "My name is Oliver McGrath, and I live over there in Horseshoe House."

Molly and Brendan told him their names. Molly said, "Our grandfather is just moving in there. "

"I look forward to meeting him," said the painter. "We can be allies."

Allies against what? Brendan wondered.

They would find out before long.

"We came out here to do a bit of exploring," said Molly.

"You didn't find the horseshoe, I suppose?"

"No, Mr McGrath," said Brendan.

"Please, call me Oliver," said the painter. "Well, never mind, you found me instead. I don't often get an audience, out here. What do you think of my work?"

He pointed at the painting. Brendan and Molly stared at it.

They could only see patches of different coloured greens, with splashes of yellow and brown here and there.

"Well . . ." said Molly. She had no idea what to

say, she didn't want to seem rude, but the picture didn't look anything like the wood they were in.

Oliver McGrath laughed. He seemed to read her thoughts. "No, it doesn't look anything like the real thing," he said. "It's not meant to. I'm trying to make a pattern, like the way the light comes through the leaves, and makes shapes of different colours. It isn't meant to be like a photograph. If it was, I'd bring a camera, instead of all this stuff."

Brendan thought he would prefer a photograph. He often took pictures himself. Some of them even came out looking blurred and patchy, a bit like Oliver's painting. But the difference was that Oliver *meant* his painting to look like that.

He tried to think of something to say, but luckily Oliver went on, "I suppose your grandfather isn't a painter, by any chance?"

"No," said Brendan, "he's more interested in horses, really."

"Yes, it's hard to paint those," said Oliver. "I had a go once but it's hard to catch the feeling of movement. At least the trees here stay still."

"I suppose we'd better get back, before they start wondering where we've got to," said Molly.

"I'll come back with you," said Oliver. "They'll be looking for me too, I expect. I'm on washing-up duty today."

Molly was startled. As Oliver began to pack up his gear, she said, "Do you have to do your own washing-up? I thought this was a luxury place."

"New routine," Oliver explained. "Since the nephew took over. They say it's to make us more self-reliant or something. Load of codswallop, if you ask me. It saves them having to pay people to do it."

"Can't you complain?" asked Brendan as they made their way through the woods back towards the house.

"What's the use? There's no one to complain to, now that Mrs Boyd is off in America. When she comes back, there'll be some complaining done, believe me!"

Outside the door of the house they met Carrie.

"Hello, Carrie," said Oliver McGrath, then he turned to Brendan and Molly and said, "she's the best of them, this one. She really seems to *like* looking after us old wrecks!"

"I *do* like it, Oliver, and you're not old wrecks," said Carrie.

"Have you met my new friends?" Oliver asked. "They've been admiring my painting." He grinned at Brendan and Molly, who smiled back, feeling guilty.

"I met them just now," said Carrie. "In fact I was coming to see where you'd both got to. Your folks are just finishing the tour of the house."

"We were exploring," said Molly.

"Good for you," said Carrie. "I hope you'll explore some more when you come and visit your grandfather. It's nice to have some young people about."

"It is," said Oliver. "Mrs Boyd used to bring some of the local schoolchildren in sometimes. They'd play games and maybe sing songs for us."

"I miss Mrs Boyd," Carrie said. "You'll really like her when you meet her."

"*If* you meet her," said Oliver gloomily.

"She will be back, won't she?" asked Molly.

"We can only hope," said Oliver.

Just then, the Boyds appeared, followed by Locky, and Brendan and Molly's mothers.

"Carrie, what are you doing standing about here?" said Maura. "There's plenty to do, isn't there?"

"Yes, Mrs Boyd," said Carrie.

"Don't blame her," said Oliver. "I kept her here chatting with these new friends I met out in the woods."

"In the woods?" said Maura sharply. "What were you doing out there?"

"We were only looking around," said Brendan. "We didn't know they were out of bounds."

Maura Boyd looked as if she was about to tell him off, but seeing the others looking at her, she gave a false smile, and said, "Of course they're not out of bounds. We just need to know where you are, that's all."

"Don't worry about those two," said Locky. "They're great kids. And I'll keep an eye on them when they come to visit, don't worry."

"Oh, we'll come and see you often, Grandpa," said Molly.

Maura Boyd didn't look very pleased at this news, but she gave her false smile again and said, "By all means, provided of course that you let us know in advance and the time is suitable."

"No problem," said Locky.

"So you're the new kid on the block," said Oliver. He introduced himself. "I'll show you around the place and tell you what's what."

"Thanks, Oliver," said Locky.

"*We* shall be able to tell you all you need to know," said Maura Boyd. Brendan saw Oliver look at Locky and make a face, behind Maura's back. Locky grinned.

"You'll enjoy it here, Mr Ryan," said Gerry Boyd. "We're one big happy family, at Horseshoe House."

"It certainly seems very comfortable," said Brendan's mother.

"I'd say you made a good choice, Dad," said Molly's mother, reluctantly. She still felt that she should have been consulted.

She went on, "Of course, it's expensive . . ."

"No doubt about that," Locky agreed. "But look on the bright side, I won't be able to squander my money on the gee-gees!"

The mothers looked disapproving. So did Maura Boyd. But she smiled, and said, "I know the fees seem a lot, but you get what you pay for. It's amazing what costs are these days. I mean, the salaries of the kitchen staff alone are huge."

"Astronomical," said Gerry Boyd. "Making all those meals, setting tables, washing up. It all costs money."

Brendan and Molly looked at each other. They knew that whatever the Boyds spent money on, it wasn't on washing up.

It looked as if the Ballygandon Private Eyes might have to do some investigating.

CHAPTER FOUR

Disappearing Dessy

"I thought Ballygandon was about as deep in the country as you could get, but this is something else!" Dessy said, as they walked from the bus stop up the drive towards Horseshoe House.

Now the summer holidays had started, Dessy and Brendan were staying with Molly for a few days in Ballygandon, where Molly's parents ran a grocery shop. On Sunday morning they caught the bus from Ballygandon to go and see Grandpa Locky. It was Dessy's first visit to Horseshoe House.

"Grandpa moved here because he wanted to, nobody forced him," said Brendan.

"But just think," said Dessy, "he could have lived in the city, with you. Imagine choosing to come to the middle of nowhere."

"The place is fine," said Molly, "or it could be, if the people running it weren't so mean. They make Grandpa and the others do their own washing up, and they've set up a kind of launderette in the basement for them to wash their own clothes as well."

"I thought you said it was meant to be a posh place," said Dessy.

"It was," said Brendan, "but the woman running it went off to California and now this pair are doing things on the cheap. They even put low wattage light-bulbs in to save money. Grandpa can't even see to read the racing pages."

"But we've got a plan to foil the Boyds there," said Molly. "I've got some higher-powered bulbs in my bag and we're going to put them in instead."

"We've got some cakes and biscuits as well," said Brendan. "They don't even give them enough to eat."

"Why don't the old folks do something about it?" Dessy asked.

"Some of them are afraid they'll be told to leave and they've nowhere else to go," said Brendan. "And Grandpa and his friend Oliver asked us not to tell our parents what the Boyds are doing just yet. I'm sure Grandpa thinks our mothers would say 'I told you so!' and insist he comes and lives with one of them."

"He and Oliver are waiting till Mrs Boyd gets back, then they'll really slam into her nephew and his wife, and show them up," said Molly. "The trouble is, no one seems to know when Mrs Boyd will come back, if she comes back at all."

"Hey, you don't suppose this new pair have done her in?" said Dessy.

Brendan and Molly looked worried. That was something they hadn't thought of. Could Gerry and Maura Boyd have murdered his aunt and only pretended she had gone to California?

Was she perhaps buried in the Monument in the

grounds of Horseshoe House? The Ballygandon Private Eyes might have more serious crimes to solve than they expected.

"Wow, that's some house!" said Dessy as they came up the drive and saw Horseshoe House ahead of them. "The people who built this certainly lived in style."

"Which is more than you can say for the people here now, like Grandpa," said Brendan, as he pulled on the bell.

The door was opened by Carrie. She seemed sniffy and tearful.

"What's the matter, Carrie?" asked Molly.

Carrie brought them into the waiting room off the hall, and closed the door. "I'll be all right," she said. "It's just the Boyds . . . they're horrible."

"What have they done now?" Brendan asked.

"I asked them for Mrs Boyd's address in America and they really snapped at me," said Carrie. "They said I had no business to be writing to her, and anyway she and her daughter were just about to move and they hadn't got the new address yet."

"A likely story," said Molly.

"They just don't want anyone telling her what's going on at Horseshoe House," said Brendan.

"Or else they're afraid you'll find out she never got there," said Dessy gloomily.

"What do you mean?" Carrie asked.

He told her in gory detail what he thought might have happened to Mrs Boyd. Carrie got very upset.

"Oh no, no! They couldn't do that!" she cried. "They're awful people, but they wouldn't go that far."

"You never know," said Dessy. He put on an

American accent and said, "Sure thing, honey, we Private Eyes dig up some dirty deeds out there in the mean streets of the city."

"It's no joking matter," said Molly.

"I ain't joking," said Dessy.

"Where's Grandpa, Carrie?" asked Brendan.

"He's in the snooker room playing darts with Oliver McGrath."

As they walked along the corridor, lined with pictures of grand-looking people in old-fashioned clothes, Dessy said, "They look a stuck-up lot."

"They're the family that used to have the house, way back when it was a big estate," said Carrie.

"What happened to that one?" asked Molly, pointing to a gap in the line of pictures.

"The Boyds have already started selling off some of the portraits," said Carrie. "They can be quite valuable."

Carrie left them at the door of the snooker room, saying she had a lot of cleaning to do. They opened the door. The room was lined with dark wood panelling and there was a snooker table in the middle. On the wall at the far end was a dart-board where Locky and Oliver were playing.

After the introductions, Locky said, "I'm glad to meet you, Dessy, I've heard a lot about you. I hear you're a bit of a humorist."

"A *bit* is right," muttered Brendan.

"I like a good joke," said Dessy. "When I grow up I want to be a stand-up comic."

"Good for you," said Locky. "What's the difference between an elephant and a letter-box?"

"I don't know," said Dessy.

"Well in that case I won't ask *you* to post a letter for me!"

Locky laughed and so did the others.

"Nice one, Mr Ryan," said Dessy.

"Call me Locky."

"OK, Locky – what do you get if you cross a kangaroo and a sheep?"

"I don't know," said Locky.

"A woolly jumper!" said Dessy.

There was laughter and Brendan said, "Dessy likes the old jokes the best."

"That wasn't all that old," said Dessy. "What do you think, Locky?"

Locky said, "No, it wasn't really old at all, Dessy. Though I must say, the first time my granny heard it, she nearly fell out of her cradle!"

There was more laughter, though Dessy's was a bit half-hearted.

"I think you've got real talent, Dessy," said Locky kindly. "But maybe we need to do a bit of practice before we launch ourselves as a double act."

"Game ball, Locky," said Dessy. "Hey, how about a game of snooker?"

"The Boyds have stopped us playing snooker," said Oliver. "They say they're afraid we'll damage the table. Personally, I think they're going to sell it."

"We've got a surprise for you, Grandpa," said Molly.

"Good girl," said Locky. "Can I see it now?"

"It's for the main living-room," said Molly. "We'll show you there."

They went through more corridors towards the front of the house, and into a large room with heavy velvet curtains and chairs and sofas all round it. There was an old television set in one corner, and small tables scattered about.

In a few of the chairs other residents of Horseshoe House were sitting, some reading, some dozing. Beside the biggest window there was a card table. Two women were sitting one on each side of it, playing a game. They were neatly dressed, one in green and the other in brown, and they each had a pearl necklace and well-groomed grey hair.

As the group came into the room one of the pair put down her cards with a flourish and said, "Gin!"

"A bit early in the day, isn't it, Harriet?" said Locky.

"You never tire of that joke, do you, Loughlin?" said Harriet. "You know very well it's a game of Gin Rummy."

"They play it all the time," Locky explained to the others.

"Let me introduce the sisters McDonald, Harriet and Brenda."

"Oh, so these are your grandchildren, Loughlin?" said Brenda.

"They are indeed. Brendan and Molly. And this is their friend Dessy, the comedian. They've come here with a surprise for me."

"Lucky you," said Harriet. "We get few surprises these days, except when Brenda wins at Gin Rummy!"

"I win just as many times as you do," said Brenda.

"No, dear," said Harriet, "you're thinking of the games of tiddly-winks we played when we were six years old. You were quite good at that."

"Indeed," said Brenda, "and I excelled at every game since then. You remember that tennis tournament at Kilkee?"

"They go on like this all the time," said Locky, "they enjoy arguing. Now, ladies, be quiet for a minute and Molly will tell us about her surprise."

"Here it is!" said Molly. She opened her bag and took out some packets of light-bulbs. "These are hundred-watt bulbs," she said. "Now you'll be able to see what you're reading in the evenings."

"Brilliant!" said Oliver.

"Brilliant in every sense," said Locky. "Let's put them in at once. The Boyds won't know until it gets dark and if they whinge about it we'll say the other ones suddenly got brighter."

They handed the bulbs to Locky and Oliver who put them in the table lamps and the tall standard lamp, but the light hanging down from the ceiling near the big window was more difficult. If they went to get a ladder it might alert the Boyds.

Brendan said, "There's a long pole over here, could we use that?"

"That's for opening the top windows," said Locky. "Yes, if we used the pole we could maybe push the flex over towards the window. I'll make sure the light's switched off first." He went over to the switch and checked it.

"I could climb up on top of that and reach over

to change it," said Dessy pointing at a huge, elaborate sideboard that stood against the wall beside the big window. He began to clamber up the shelves that formed the top part of the gigantic piece of furniture. The shelves were empty, though at one time they had held ornaments and plates and dishes and glass. Once more the Boyds had found something to sell off.

Dessy was soon on top of the sideboard, lying flat and almost hidden by the piece of carved wood that jutted out around the top.

Brendan took the window-pole and poked it up towards the hanging light. He brought it nearly across to the sideboard.

Molly climbed up and handed Dessy the hundred-watt bulb. He put it down beside him, and reached out for the hanging bulb.

He leaned out, and nearly overbalanced and fell. But finally he got hold of it, and took the bulb out of the holder. Carefully he put the new bulb in, and Brendan guided the flex back to its original place, hanging from the ceiling.

The residents who weren't asleep clapped their hands, which woke up the ones who were asleep. Locky went to the light switch beside the door and said, "Now, watch this. Abracadabra, let there be LIGHT!"

He flicked the switch and all the bulbs glowed on. Even in the daylight, it was clear that they were powerful. Everyone applauded again.

Locky turned the switch off, saying with a grin, "We'll save them till tonight. We don't want to waste electricity, do we?"

He was just in time. At that moment the door opened and Maura Boyd came in, followed by Gerry. At once, all the residents pretended things were as usual. The McDonald sisters started a new game of Gin Rummy, the readers went back to their papers, and the sleepers pretended to go back to sleep.

Oliver went over to the window. "Hello, Gerry, hello Maura," he said. "I was just showing Locky's grandchildren the view from here and how I plan to paint it. You see the way the light falls on the woods there . . ."

"Yes, yes, Mr McGrath," said Gerry, "we all know you're the bee's knees when it comes to painting, even if we can't tell what your pictures are meant to be."

"Good morning, Mr Boyd," said Brendan with fake politeness.

"Good morning, Mrs Boyd," said Molly.

"Good morning," said Maura Boyd, icily. "And where is your friend?"

"Friend?" Molly looked innocent.

"Yes, friend," said Maura impatiently. "I was upstairs and saw the three of you walking up the drive. Where is the other boy?"

"I don't know," said Brendan.

"Up to some mischief I expect," said Maura. "You can't leave children unsupervised."

"Probably playing hide-and-seek or some such caper," said Gerry. "In which case you can tell him to come out now."

"He's . . . he's out, looking at the flowers," said Harriet McDonald.

"A likely story," said Maura Boyd. "I'm sure he's hiding in here somewhere. And I shall find him."

Brendan tried his best not to look at the sideboard, but he just couldn't stop himself having a quick glance upwards. He was relieved to find that Dessy wasn't visible. He must be lying quite flat on the top there. Unfortunately, Maura Boyd had seen his glance.

"So, he's up there, is he?" she snapped. "Well, we'll soon have him down. How dare he go climbing over this valuable furniture? Boy! Come down at once! Boy! Do you hear me?"

There was silence. Maura Boyd looked around at the group.

The McDonald sisters smiled sweetly at her. Oliver shrugged. Locky made a face. The others simply gazed back at her or pretended to be asleep. Molly and Brendan glanced at each other, nervously.

"Gerald!" Maura Boyd said to her husband. "Climb up and flush him out!"

Gerry Boyd looked hesitant. Then he said, "Very well, my love, if you say so." He dragged a chair across to the sideboard, climbed on to it, grunting, and then on to the main shelf of the sideboard. When he stood on tiptoe he was able to peer over the top. Molly and Brendan prepared for disaster.

But Gerry Boyd turned and announced, "There's nothing up here. Nothing at all."

Brendan and Molly stared at each other. Dessy had disappeared into thin air!

CHAPTER FIVE

Sinister Plans

"Right then, you two, where is he?" Maura Boyd snapped at Brendan and Molly.

"I don't know," said Brendan. He wished he did. Whatever could have become of Dessy?

"Well, you'd better find him, and when you do, it's time all three of you went home. Come along, Gerry."

Gerry Boyd was dusting himself off after his climb up the sideboard. "I'm coming," he said. The Boyds strode out of the room.

As the door shut behind them, Molly went to the sideboard and called up, "Dessy, where are you? Are you all right?"

"Fine. But I can't hang around here much longer!" Dessy's voice came from behind the long thick curtain on the window beside the sideboard. Brendan pulled the edge of the curtain aside. There was Dessy, hanging by his hands from the curtain rail, supporting himself with one foot on a lamp bracket jutting from the wall.

"Hang on, Dessy, we'll get you down," said Molly.

"Here, use this table," said Brenda McDonald. The sisters got up and pulled their card table over to the curtain.

"We'll put a chair on top, and have him down in a jiffy," said Locky. He put one of the chairs on top of the table. Brendan scrambled up and stood on the chair and held on to Dessy as he let go of the rail and dropped down beside him.

They both got down. Everyone clapped. Dessy took a bow.

"You're quite a gymnast, Dessy," said Oliver.

"I'm working on it," said Dessy. "I didn't think my arms would hold out. When I realised they were coming up to look on top, the only thing I could think of was to get behind the curtain and grab the rail."

"Well, you had us fooled," said Locky. "We were sure they were going to find you."

"I suppose we'd better head off, before the Boyds find we're still here," said Brendan.

"Come and see us again soon," said Locky. "And thanks for fixing the lights – at least we'll be able to see to read now."

"And you'll be able to see your cards properly, Brenda," said Harriet McDonald.

"My eyes are just as good as yours," said Brenda.

"Then why did you mistake that Queen for a King last time?"

Molly grinned. If the McDonald sisters were starting to bicker again, then everything was back to normal.

When they were outside the front door, Brendan

looked at his watch. "There's an hour before the next bus," he said.

"Let's go into the wood and have another look at the monument," said Molly.

"Yes, maybe we'll find that horseshoe," said Dessy.

They went all round the monument, pulling aside the ivy to look under it, and feeling the stones and marble slabs to see if any of them were loose.

"Hey, why don't we climb up on top there and see what we can see?" said Brendan.

"OK, and this time it's your turn to do the climbing," said Dessy.

"No problem," Brendan said, and began to grab the ivy and pull himself up. Molly and Dessy cupped their hands so he could push on them with his feet. Then he was able to step on Dessy's shoulder and heave himself up over the ridge of battlements.

From the ground, the battlements hid Brendan from their view. Molly called out, "Can you see anything up there?"

"There's just a flat stone roof, with moss and ivy and stuff on it," said Brendan. He began to crawl along it, lifting the ivy here and there.

"No horseshoes?" asked Molly.

"No sign of one, yet."

"Hey," said Dessy, "I've just thought of a good one. Why is a pony like someone with a sore throat?"

Molly sighed. "I've no idea, Dessy."

"They're both a little hoarse!" said Dessy. Molly raised her eyes in mock despair. "HORSE – gee-gee, HOARSE – sore throat, get it?" Dessy went on.

"Yes, Dessy, we get it," said Molly.

"Hang on," said Brendan, "I can see over to the house, through the trees there."

"And . . . ?" said Molly.

"At the back there's a sort of wooden out-house. Like a big shed. And Locky and Oliver have started to paint it green."

"What are they doing that for?" asked Dessy.

"I don't know," said Brendan. "Maybe they wanted to."

"Don't be an eejit," said Molly.

"Well, Oliver likes painting," said Brendan.

"Not that kind of painting, he's artistic," said Molly.

"Maybe the Boyds told them to do it," suggested Dessy.

"I reckon that's right," said Brendan. "Mrs Boyd has just come out to look at them. She's pointing at the shed and telling them what to do."

"I'm surprised they don't slosh the paint all over her," said Dessy.

"I'm sure they'd love to," said Molly. "But I think they're going along with her nonsense for now. Grandpa's house is sold, so he can't go back there. They're biding their time till they can get their revenge and boot out the Boyds for good."

"We've got to try to help them," said Dessy.

"Wait!" said Brendan. "Maura Boyd has left them. She's coming into the woods. She seems to be coming this way."

"Get down, quick!" said Molly. Brendan scrambled over the battlements at the edge of the roof and they helped him down to the ground.

"Why is she coming here?" asked Dessy.

"I don't know," said Molly, "but we can't get away now without her seeing us. We'll just have to keep out of sight behind the monument."

They crouched down, waiting. They could hear the crack of branches as Maura Boyd made her way through the wood.

She came to the monument.

Then they heard her say, with an unpleasant laugh, "The Horseshoe House monument. What a monstrosity! Well, we won't have to look at it much longer!"

On the far side of the monument the three listeners glanced at each other. What was Mrs Boyd planning? There was silence. Molly whispered, "I'm going to creep round and see what she's doing."

"Don't let her see you," said Brendan.

Molly tiptoed round the side of the monument. She was able to peer through some ivy which stuck out at the corner. Mrs Boyd was sitting on the steps of the monument and staring out into the woods. Then she looked at her watch.

Brendan and Dessy were crouched down just behind Molly.

"What's happening?" Dessy whispered.

Molly leaned down to them and said very softly, "I think she's waiting for somebody." Just then they heard more cracking of branches. Molly turned back to peer through the ivy.

She saw a man with a smart tweed cap on his head approaching. "Mr Murphy?" asked Mrs Boyd.

"The very same," said the man. "Mixer Murphy,

42

they call me. I'm the fastest concrete mixer in Ireland, and when there's trouble, I can mix it with the best!"

"I'm Maura Boyd. You took your time, didn't you?" She pointed at her watch.

"Well, if you *will* choose an outlandish spot like this for a meeting, what can you expect?" The man had a deep, booming voice.

Mrs Boyd said "Keep your voice down. The reason we're out in the wood is that I don't want the people in the house to know we're meeting."

"Fair enough," said Mixer Murphy. "OK, what's your proposition?"

"I've sketched out some plans," said Maura Boyd. Molly saw her take some folded papers from inside her jacket. She opened them out and held them so Mixer Murphy could see them.

After a while he said, "That's quite a job you're planning."

"If you're interested, we can talk money terms."

"Oh, I'm interested all right. But listen, I've made a few inquiries and I gather this place belongs to your husband's aunt. Does she know about this?"

"She's gone away to the States. But it's all sorted out. She gave us full power to run the place and do what we felt was needed."

"What a sensible lady she is," said Mixer Murphy with a grin. "Or a rash one, according to your point of view."

Maura·Boyd looked annoyed. "Are you interested, or not?"

"I said I was, didn't I? I'd need to see the

documents handing things over to you, of course. Just a formality, you understand." -

"You'll see them."

"Good. Well, Mrs Boyd, I think we can do business. Now, supposing we walk the land a bit and then I can see just what might be involved."

"Right. This way." She began to walk straight towards the corner of the Monument where Molly was hidden.

Molly turned and whispered, "Quick, move!" They crept back along the side of the Monument and darted round the corner just as Mrs Boyd and Mixer Murphy appeared. They could see the pair of them walking off into the wood, through the clearing where they had first seen Oliver painting.

"She's up to no good, that's obvious," said Molly.

"I wonder what those plans were?" said Dessy.

"And what did she mean about the monument?" Brendan asked. "It sounded as if she's going to pull it down."

"Maybe she plans to pull down more than the monument," said Molly.

"Whatever she's planning, things don't look good for Grandpa and his new home," said Brendan.

"Who is this Mixer Murphy guy?" asked Dessy.

"I'll ask my father if he knows about him," said Brendan. "He's a journalist, they get to find out about people."

Brendan told his father he had heard rumours that plans were being made for the school, involving a man called Mixer Murphy.

His father was quite upset.

"That wheeler-dealer!" he exclaimed. "The less they have to do with him, the better. He's only just escaped being jailed for some of his dubious deals. I'd better go and ask the school authorities what they're playing at."

"No, no, Dad," said Brendan hastily. "It's only a rumour. I don't expect there's anything in it."

"Well, you tell me if you hear any more of these rumours!"

"I will, Dad. But what does he do, this Mixer Murphy?"

"He's a builder and property developer, or that's what he calls himself. Totally ruthless when it comes to buying up land and old houses and pulling them down – often before he's even got planning permission."

Brendan was alarmed. Out in the park that evening, he told Dessy what his father had said.

"That Murphy guy sounds like a right crook," said Dessy.

"We've got to find out more about what the Boyds are up to," said Brendan, "then if only we knew where Mrs Boyd is in California, we could warn her about what's going on."

"Let's hope she *is* somewhere in California," said Dessy, "and not six feet under ground!"

CHAPTER SIX

Computer Clues

A few days later Brendan and Dessy were back staying with Molly in Ballygandon. The three of them were going to visit Locky. As they walked up the drive to Horseshoe House, they saw Carrie coming towards them. She was carrying a suitcase and looking sad and tearful. What was odder still was the sight of Locky, Oliver and the McDonald sisters walking behind Carrie, also looking very sad.

"Carrie, what's the matter, what's happened?" asked Molly, as Carrie reached them.

"They've sacked me," Carrie said, her voice breaking.

"No!" Brendan couldn't believe it.

"They have indeed," said Locky. "That pair of skinflints said they couldn't afford to keep Carrie on."

"*And* they said her work wasn't good enough," said Oliver. "The cheek of it! She's the best carer in the whole place."

"They even accused her of changing the light

bulbs," said Locky. "We told them *we'd* done it, but they took no notice."

"We'll miss you, Carrie," said Brenda McDonald. "You're our friend!"

Carrie burst into tears. Molly gave her a hug.

"We tried to protest to the Boyds, and get them to keep her," said Harriet, "but they took no notice of us at all."

"So the least we could do is come and see her off on the bus," said Oliver.

"You'll be back, Carrie, believe me," said Locky, "just as soon as we get rid of these horrible people. Imagine saying they can't afford to pay Carrie, when we all pay a fortune to stay here!"

"Not to mention getting us to wash up, and paint sheds, and do our own laundry," said Oliver. "There's something very fishy going on, if you ask me."

"And we think we've got an idea what it might be," said Brendan.

He explained what they had seen and heard in the wood. Then they saw the bus approaching.

"Thanks, thanks for everything," Carrie said, as she prepared to get on. She handed Locky a piece of paper. "That's my home address," she said. "Let me know how you get on."

"Don't worry, we'll be seeing you back here soon, Carrie!" said Locky.

Carrie smiled and waved, and they all waved back as the bus pulled away.

Back at the house, they had a conference in the sitting-room.

"If we could find those papers Maura Boyd showed Mixer Murphy," said Brendan, "we'd know more about what they're planning."

"We'll form a search party," said Locky. "I think I know where the papers might be."

He told them the Boyds' office was next to the waiting room off the hallway. It had a big desk against the window, with a computer on it, as well as a telephone and wire trays with letters and papers in them.

"Those papers must be somewhere in that desk," said Locky.

"But how could you hunt there without being seen?" asked Harriet McDonald.

"I've got an idea," said Oliver. "I saw Gerry Boyd drive off into town not long ago, so that just leaves Maura. Why don't I tell her I want some advice about the shed we're painting, then lock her inside it?"

"There'll be hell to pay when she comes out," said Brenda.

"I don't care, I'll just pretend it was an accident," said Oliver.

He went out of the room.

Soon afterwards, they heard him talking to Maura Boyd in the hallway. Brendan opened the door a fraction and peeped through. Maura Boyd was standing facing Oliver, her hands on her hips.

"But I told you what to do with the shed, why don't you just get on with it?" she snapped.

"Well, it's a question of the finish," said Oliver, "we do want to get it just right, the way you want it. If you could just come out for a moment and have a look . . ."

"Oh, very well," Maura Boyd grumbled. "Come along, then!"

She strode to the front door, opened it and went out. Oliver followed and as he went through the door he turned and saw the sitting-room door ajar. He grinned and gave the thumbs-up sign, then closed the front door behind him.

"OK, let's go!" said Locky. He and Brendan and Molly and Dessy went out into the hallway, leaving the others to keep an eye on the front door in case Oliver's scheme failed and Maura Boyd came back.

"This is the office," said Locky. He tried the door and it opened. There across the room was the big desk he had described.

They went over to it. First they looked through the papers in the wire trays, but they seemed to be mainly bills and letters.

They tried the drawers. The top ones contained pens and writing paper and stamps and a black leather-covered book with ADDRESSES stamped on it in gold letters.

"Look at this," said Brendan. "Maybe we can find Mrs Boyd's daughter's address in California." He turned to the B section. "Yes, here it is. It says *Helen Boyd*, and then *Warren* in brackets. That must be her married name. It's an address in Los Angeles. But there's no phone number."

"I'll copy the address down," said Molly. "Then we can write to her." She took a piece of paper and began writing the address down.

"Didn't the Boyds say she was moving?" asked Dessy.

"I think that was just a lie, to put Carrie off," said Brendan. "But if not, they'll surely forward it." He put back the address book and they went on searching for the papers about the plans.

Another drawer had a small bottle of whiskey in it, and a packet of biscuits.

"Great! I'm hungry," said Dessy reaching for it.

"Don't be an eejit," said Molly. "They'll notice you've been at the packet."

"Do you think they count them?" Dessy asked.

"Well, *you* do!" said Brendan.

"OK," said Dessy, "hands off the biscuits."

"*And* the whiskey!" said Locky.

"Never touch the stuff," said Dessy.

There was a last drawer at the bottom, on the left hand side of the desk. It was locked.

"Shall we break it open?" Brendan suggested.

"They'd notice that, all right," said Locky. "Maybe they've got the key hidden somewhere."

They began hunting round on the shelves and looking in plant-pots. Then Brendan said, "I know! We'll try the computer! Maybe the stuff is in there somewhere."

"I never got the hang of those things," said Locky.

"Brendan's quite a whizz-kid," said Dessy.

"Well, I'll have a go," said Brendan, pleased.

Soon he had the computer switched on and had brought up a list of files on the screen.

There were the names of the residents of

Horseshoe House, and the staff, and files labelled PLUMBER, ELECTRICITY, COUNCIL, and so on.

"That doesn't look very promising," said Locky.

"Wait a minute," said Brendan. "What about this? There's a file called DOUBLE M."

Sounds like a ranch," said Dessy. "SHOWDOWN AT THE DOUBLE M STOCKADE!"

Brendan ignored him. "DOUBLE M," he said. "MM. That could stand for Mixer Murphy." He pressed the key to get access to the file. On to the screen came a page of print headed:

HORSESHOE HOUSE: DEVELOPMENT PLAN

"That's it!" said Molly.

She and the others leaned over Brendan's shoulder to look at the screen. The plan listed details of the various buildings and woods and fields of the Horseshoe House estate, and what would happen to them.

"Well it looks as if they're saving the House itself," said Brendan.

"But not the residents!" Locky exclaimed. "It says *House to be developed as high-class Health Centre.*"

"And then it says *Bank loan agreed for twenty-five luxury homes to be built on estate,*" said Molly. "How would they find space to build them?"

"By cutting down most of the trees," said Locky.

"And look at this!" said Brendan. *"Out-houses and external sheds, buildings, and greenhouse to be dismantled. Other unnecessary buildings in grounds, including Monument, to be destroyed."*

"It's vandalism, that's what it is!" said Locky angrily.

Brendan scrolled on to the next page on the screen. It showed drawings of Horseshoe House and the estate and where the houses would be. They worked out that one of the houses stood exactly on the site of the monument.

"I suppose the Boyds are hiring Mixer Murphy to do all this," said Locky.

"And do you think Mrs Boyd really gave Gerry and Maura permission to do what they liked with the place?" asked Dessy.

"I doubt it," said Locky.

"But Maura said she'd show Mixer the documents," said Molly.

"She's probably forged them," said Locky.

"Yes, look at this!" said Brendan. He had moved on to the next page on the screen. It was headed:

HORSESHOE HOUSE: OWNERSHIP AGREEMENT

It was all written in legal language, but it definitely said that Mrs Laura Boyd gave all rights and powers over the House and estate to her nephew Gerry Boyd and his wife Maura.

"They must have made this up themselves," said Locky. "Otherwise, it wouldn't be in the same file with the plans. I'm sure Mrs Boyd knows nothing about any of it."

They heard the front door slam. "That may be Maura Boyd, we must get out, quick!" whispered Locky urgently. Brendan closed down the computer and they all rushed to the door.

They were met by Oliver who said breathlessly, "Hurry! I locked her in, but she's battering at the door of the shed. I'm sure she'll break out any minute."

They all rushed down the hallway, into the living room, and closed the door behind them. Locky and Oliver quickly sat down in chairs and began reading magazines, while Brendan, Molly and Dessy went into the far corner of the room and sat in a circle on the floor. Dessy produced some dice and they started a game.

Soon the door was flung open and Maura Boyd stormed in. She went across to Oliver and shouted, "You idiot! You thick-headed geriatric dolt!" She went on for a while, swearing and cursing at Oliver, who just kept gazing up at her, looking mildly puzzled.

When she finally paused for breath, Oliver said, "I'm sorry, Mrs Boyd, what seems to be the problem?"

Dessy started to chuckle, then put his hand over his mouth.

"You locked me in the shed, you bone-headed twit!" shrieked Maura Boyd.

"Oh, my goodness gracious me!" said Oliver, pretending to be distressed. "What a very silly fellow I am. I must have locked the door by mistake. I'm so, so sorry . . ."

"So you should be, you moronic old fool!" snapped Maura. Then she noticed all the others gazing at the scene with interest and barked, "And what are you lot staring at? You useless bunch of fogeys!" With that she turned and marched out of the room, slamming the door.

"Dear, dear," said Locky, "temper, temper! Well done, Oliver. Now let me tell you what Brendan found out . . ."

When they had given Oliver the news, Locky said, "I've just thought of a way we might stall their plans until we can get hold of Mrs Boyd and put a stop to them for good."

He went on to tell them that a friend of his worked in the Historical Preservation section of one of the Government ministries. She was one of the experts in charge of listing old buildings of historical importance which no one was allowed to change or pull down.

"I'll give her a call," said Locky. "She'll be able to tell us if that monument in the grounds is listed to be preserved."

When Locky came back from telephoning he said, "Gemma says she'll have to look up the records and if the monument is listed, she can give us copies of the documents. She should have them by tomorrow."

"If only we could get them right away," said Oliver. "By the time the post arrives, the Boyds may rush ahead with their plans, and Mixer Murphy's bulldozers will be moving in."

"She won't be able to come down here with them tomorrow," said Locky. "There's a big race meeting on and she's going to it. A great horse-race fan is Gemma – like myself."

"Well, there's no time to lose," said Brendan. "Let's all go up to the Races and meet her there!"

CHAPTER SEVEN

Adventures at the Races

On the train from Ballygandon, Brendan leaned out of the window as they came to the station where Locky should be waiting. Locky had given them the money for their fares, saying he was sure he would win it back at the races.

"There he is!" Brendan called.

Locky was waiting on the platform. With him were Oliver and the McDonald sisters.

"We thought we'd all come along, we like a bit of a flutter," said Harriet McDonald as they all climbed on to the train.

"The more the merrier," said Locky.

They settled down in their seats, and Molly produced a bag of sandwiches and handed them round.

Brenda McDonald said, "We wanted to bring some food too, but they lock up everything in the kitchen at Horseshoe House."

"Never mind," said Locky, "I'll buy you all a banquet with my winnings!"

"Did you have any problem getting away, Grandpa?" asked Brendan.

"We didn't tell the Boyds we were going," said Locky, "and anyway, they were too busy walking around the estate with that developer fellow to notice us leaving."

"We asked the taxi to wait at the end of the drive," Oliver explained, "just in case they saw us getting into it to go to the station."

"Oh, there'll be hell to pay when they find out we've gone," said Harriet McDonald, gleefully.

"We'll be sent to bed with no supper!" giggled her sister.

Brendan thought they were like a bunch of kids, thrilled to be off on a forbidden adventure.

At the racecourse they joined the crowds going through the turnstiles. Inside, there was a large open area with booths selling race-cards and guides to form, as well as hot dogs and snacks.

On either side of the area were two big grandstands, with sloping terraces and rows of seats. In front of the stands there was a forest of wooden boards on poles, with names and numbers on them.

"They're the bookies' stands," said Locky, "and those are the bookies themselves in front of them, writing up the odds they're giving on the different horses."

"It's the bookies who really make the money at this game," said Oliver.

"And today I mean to make some money too!" said Locky. "The first race is coming up, and I've got a certainty. Texas Gem will romp home. Wait here just a minute." He disappeared into the crowd, towards the bookies' stands.

"We'll go and buy us all some tickets for the special enclosure, there'll be more room there," said Oliver. He and the McDonald sisters went away towards one of the booths.

"I wish we had enough money to put on some bets," said Dessy.

"Let's make some!" said Molly.

"How?"

Molly pointed to a bearded man with a floppy black hat who was sitting in the middle of the open area. He was playing a *bodhrán*, and a few people were standing around listening. In front of him on the ground was a box with some coins in it.

"Busking," said Molly. "That's the way to earn a bob or two."

She went across to the *bodhrán* player and produced her tin whistle. "Mind if I join in?" she asked.

Brendan was afraid the musician would tell Molly to get off his patch, but he just smiled and said, "Play away, girl."

So Molly began to play a reel and the *bodhrán* player drummed away vigorously. People were tapping their feet, and Dessy even tried a few step-dance moves, but then tripped and stumbled.

"You're not quite ready for *Riverdance* yet," Brendan grinned.

Molly and the *bodhrán* player did another couple of numbers and a small crowd gathered. When she finished there was applause, and the musician said, "Well done, girl. You're good."

"Thanks," said Molly. "And thanks for letting me play."

"You deserve some of this," said the man, picking up the box, which had got a lot more coins in it since Molly had joined him. He scooped up a handful of the coins and gave them to Molly.

"See you again," he said. "Keep playing."

"There you are!" said Locky, coming up to them. "I wondered where you'd got to."

"We were just earning a bit of cash for the betting," said Dessy.

"We?" said Brendan, laughing.

"Well, as Molly's manager, naturally I get a cut," said Dessy.

"Well done, anyway," said Locky. "Now where have Oliver and those McDonald girls gone? We'll miss the first race if we don't hurry."

Just then Oliver appeared clutching the badges for the special enclosure. They all put them on and went through another gate.

"Shall we go up in the grandstand?" asked Harriet McDonald.

"You go if you like," said Locky. "I'd rather go and watch it close to, from the fence there."

Oliver and the McDonald sisters climbed the stairs to take seats in the stand. Locky and the others moved through the crowd till they came to a white metal railing. Right in front of them was the grass of the race-track itself, and opposite on the far side was the winning post.

Just beside it there was a giant video screen and on it they could see the horses moving around while they waited for the start of the race. In the distance, further down the track, they could see the actual horses that were pictured on the screen. A wire was drawn tight across the track to keep them back.

"There's mine, number four, Texas Gem!" said Locky, pointing at a horse on the screen. It was grey and was ridden by a jockey wearing a red and white striped outfit and a red spotted hat.

"What odds did you get?" asked Dessy.

"Fifteen to one," said Locky.

"That means he'll get fifteen pounds for every pound he puts on," Dessy explained.

"Yes, we *had* worked that out, as a matter of fact, Dessy," said Brendan sarcastically.

"How much did you bet, Grandpa?" Molly asked.

"A fiver," said Locky. "So I stand to gain seventy-five quid."

"Phew!" said Dessy.

The horses were lining up in front of the stretched wire. The commentator on the loudspeakers said, "They're off!" as the wire dropped and the horses leaped forward.

Locky pulled a pair of binoculars out and peered down the track.

"Here they come!" he said, as the horses raced past them, their hooves thudding on the turf.

"Texas Gem is out in front already!" cried Brendan.

"Let's hope he stays there," said Locky, gazing through his binoculars as the horses went on into the distance round the curve of the track.

Inside the rail, a van with a camera was speeding

along just in front of the horses, so the spectators could see the close-up picture on the video screen. In the far distance they could see the white rails going up a slight hill, and the group of horses pounding along.

"And as they come to the halfway mark," said the commentator, "it's Mountfern Mary in the lead, followed by Heronsgate, with Texas Gem in third place . . ."

"Come on, Texas Gem!" shouted Brendan and Molly and Dessy together.

"I hope he can hear you," said Locky. The race went on, with the three horses neck and neck. Then Heronsgate stumbled and the jockey fell off. He got up, but the horse had gone on with the race, even without his rider.

Now they could see the real horses in the distance, as they approached the last stretch. "And it's Mountfern Mary and Texas Gem battling it out for first place!" said the commentator excitedly. The crowd of spectators began to roar and cheer, as the horses thundered towards them.

"And at the finish, it's Texas Gem by a short head!" shouted the commentator as the crowd's roar reached a peak.

"She's done it!" said Locky triumphantly, as his three friends jumped up and down, shrieking with delight.

Locky collected his winnings and treated them all to fish and chips and hamburgers and ice creams. Molly asked him to put two pounds of her money on a horse called Teenage Werewolf.

"It must win, it must!" chanted Molly as they waited for the race.

"With a name like that it will probably frighten all the others away," said Dessy. "Hey, do you know what the Werewolf said when it came to dinner and bit everyone at the table?"

"No, Dessy," said Brendan.

"Fangs for the meal!" said Dessy.

"They're off!" called the commentator, and they all turned to watch the race.

Teenage Werewolf came an easy first and Molly began to feel hoarse from all the cheering she had done. She won twelve pounds and said it was her turn to treat them.

Locky said he had arranged to meet his friend Gemma by the rails, opposite the winning post, before the third race started.

"Here she comes!" said Locky. They saw coming towards them a tall woman in a smart check coat. She had black hair and a wide green straw hat. She was carrying a brief-case.

"Hello there, Locky," she said, smiling.

"Gemma!" said Locky. "How are you?"

There were introductions and Gemma said, "So you are the young people who are keeping a watch on our ancient buildings." She opened her brief-case and took out some documents.

"That monument is more than two hundred years old," she said. "There is no way anyone would be allowed to mess about with it. Here are copies of the historical papers about it, and the preservation order. You can show them to those people at Horseshoe House."

"I hope they'll take some notice," said Molly.

"Well, if they don't, we'll have the law on them," said Gemma. "If they look like being difficult, just let me know and I'll come down and sort them out."

"Oh, they're difficult, all right," said Brendan.

"Yes, if they want to do something, they'll go ahead and do it," said Locky. "They're quite ruthless."

"They aren't even scared of the Phantom Horseman," said Dessy.

"Who's he?" asked Gemma.

They told her about the legend and the story of the lost horseshoe. "Well, if it will save the place, let's hope you find it," said Gemma.

"Meanwhile," said Locky, "have you got any good tips?"

"There's a young hopeful I fancy in the fifth," said Gemma seriously. She produced her race programme and she and Locky studied it, talking earnestly about form and jockeys and weights and odds.

"Let's take a wander around the place," said Brendan.

They walked away from the track and round to the back of the stands. They saw the Parade Ring where the horses came before the race and paraded round so that the spectators could see them close to. Beyond it was the weighing room, and a building with high windows. Through them they could see saddles and jockeys' hats hanging up.

"That must be where they change into their gear,"

said Brendan. They walked towards the building and went round the side of it. There was a door and some benches outside it, not far from the race-track railing. Brendan thought they must be for jockeys to sit and watch races they weren't in. There was no one on the benches now, so the three of them sat down.

"I'd really fancy being a jockey," said Molly. "It must be fantastically exciting."

"And you'd look good in the outfit," said Brendan.

"We all would," said Dessy, "I just fancy myself in one of those bright silk shirts!"

"Maybe this is your chance," said Brendan. "Look there."

He pointed to one of the benches near the door to the jockey's changing room. There was a bulging hold-all on it.

"Someone must have left it behind," said Molly. She went across and picked it up. She brought it over and put it down on the bench beside them and unzipped it.

Sure enough, inside there was a folded jockey's outfit, white pants, purple and green silk shirt and cap, with goggles and a riding crop too. And at the bottom in a clear plastic bag there was a pair of riding-boots.

"Go on, Molly, you try it on," said Brendan. "You're the rider."

"Do you think I should?"

"Why not?" said Dessy. "It's only borrowing it for a while. The jockey can't need it, or he wouldn't have left it lying around."

Molly went round the corner behind the changing-room building. Before long she appeared again, dressed in the full jockey's gear.

"Wow!" said Brendan.

"Gee-up!" said Dessy.

"You actually do look like a real jockey," said Brendan. "I wish we had a camera."

Molly pulled the cap down and put the goggles over her eyes. She took the riding crop she'd found in the bag, and pretended to whack a horse with it, holding imaginary reins in her other hand.

Suddenly, the door of the changing room opened, and a jockey in full gear came out. Seeing Molly he said, "Ready, Joe? They're in the ring already." The jockey moved on, round the corner of the building, towards the Parade Ring.

Seeing the outfit, he'd assumed it was the jockey called Joe wearing it. Then, all at once, a bunch of other jockeys came out of the door and started off towards the Parade Ring, hurrying Molly along with them.

She looked back at Brendan and Dessy, but there was nothing to be done.

"What shall we do?" asked Brendan anxiously.

"We could always put on a bet!" said Dessy, as they hurried after the jockeys towards the Parade Ring.

CHAPTER EIGHT

The Mystery Jockey

The horses were being led around the Parade Ring by stable lads and girls. One by one the jockeys climbed on to them and walked them round the ring.

Molly kept her head down so that the cap and goggles would hide her face. Then she heard the girl leading one of the horses say, "On you get, Joe." The horse had the number five on its saddle. Molly scrambled on, and put her feet in the stirrups. They seemed very high so that her knees bent more than she was used to in her ordinary riding.

The stable girl said, "Good luck, La Signora!" and patted the light brown flank of the horse. Molly took the reins gently and let the horse walk round the ring. She still kept her head down, hoping no one would notice she wasn't Joe. But the purple and green outfit seemed to fool everyone.

Where was Joe, the real jockey? If he didn't appear, perhaps she would find herself out there on the race-track, galloping along with the other horses and riders. She would have to do something before that happened. As she moved round the ring, she passed Brendan and Dessy standing by the rail. They grinned and gave the thumbs up sign.

A fat lot of help that was, Molly thought. She wondered what would happen to her when she was found out.

She heard raised voices over at the entrance to the Parade Ring. She looked across and saw a group of people chattering agitatedly. They were looking across the ring at her. In the middle of them was a small man in a tee-shirt and red boxer shorts. He was pointing at La Signora, and he seemed very angry.

"That's *my* horse!" she heard him shout, "and my clothes! Get that thief off there!"

He strode towards Molly, shaking his fist. "Get off! Get off!" he cried. The shouts frightened La Signora who reared up on her hind legs.

Molly held on to the reins and said, "Quiet, pet, quiet!" The horse put its front legs down again, but then it trotted to the rail and jumped over it, out of the Parade Ring. The spectators scattered. There were screams and shouts. Molly realised she would have to try to get the horse away from the crowds if she was going to calm it down.

She turned the horse and got her to trot towards the dressing room building. When she'd got her round the back, she reined La Signora in. Brendan and Dessy had rushed after her. Quickly Molly dismounted and gave the reins to them.

"Hold on to her!" she said. Brendan grabbed the reins and on the other side of the horse's head,

66

Dessy took hold of the bridle. Together they managed to hold the horse still, while Molly vanished behind the building where she'd left her clothes.

Soon the jockey Joe appeared with several other people. "There she is! Grab her!" he shouted.

Brendan thought they meant Molly, but she was nowhere to be seen. He realised Joe was talking about La Signora. As the stable girl came over and took hold of the horse she said sharply, "Who are *you*?"

"We were just passing," said Brendan, "when the horse came round the corner. So we got hold of it."

"And where's the rider?" snapped Joe.

"What rider?" said Dessy innocently.

"That impostor in my clothes!" said Joe. "He can't have gone far. Find him!" By now a lot of other people had followed them from the Parade Ring, keen to see what was happening.

They all began rushing about and in the general hubbub, Brendan saw Molly slip out from behind the building and join the crowd of searchers. She had changed back into her own clothes. No one recognised her as the false jockey.

"Nice work, Molly," said Brendan softly. "You really looked the part."

"Here! They're over here!" someone called. The pile of Joe's clothes had been found. Joe snatched them and disappeared into the changing room.

They waited till he came out again, and got into the saddle on La Signora. He walked the horse back to join the others, who were now moving from the

Parade Ring and on to the race-track. Beside the rails they found Locky and Gemma, studying the race programme. Then Locky took his binoculars and gazed at the horses as they went towards the starting line.

"I fancy La Signora for this one," said Dessy.

"Ah-ha, a tipster!" said Gemma. "Do you know that horse?"

"No," said Dessy, "but Molly does – very well indeed."

"Well, I've just got time to put a bet on," said Gemma, and hurried across to the bookies' area.

When the horses reached the final stretch, there was La Signora, a length ahead of the field.

"She's won!" they all shouted as the horse streaked past the winning post.

They were just about to go over with Gemma to collect her winnings when they heard a familiar voice cry, "Oh no! I don't believe this!"

It was Brendan's father. He came striding over to their group. He had a notebook in his hand. Brendan realised he must be writing about the races for the newspaper.

"Well, hello there, Pat!" said Locky cheerily.

"So this is where you are!" Brendan's father sounded angry. "That woman at Horseshoe House has been ringing us since this morning, saying you and three of the other people took off without saying a word to anyone. She was furious!"

"I'm sure she was," said Locky, delighted.

"Locky, you'll go too far one of these days," said Mr O'Hara. "You're totally irresponsible." He stared at Brendan and went on, "And what are you doing here? You're not old enough."

"Oh, I don't know about that," said Locky. "I'm nearly seventy, after all."

"Not *you*, Locky – the children!"

"It's not Grandpa's fault," said Brendan. "We suggested coming."

"You see, Uncle Pat," Molly explained. "Grandpa had to meet Mrs Danaher, because she knows about old buildings, and she was finding out about the monument at Horseshoe House, because the Boyds are planning to knock it down . . ."

"Stop, Molly, stop!" said Mr O'Hara. "I don't know who's planning what at Horseshoe House, but there's a right panic going on there just now. I want you to ring them and tell them you're on your way back." He took a mobile phone out of his pocket and handed it to Locky.

"OK," said Locky, and dialled the number. He was smooth and polite. "Oh, hello there, Mrs Boyd, this is Loughlin Ryan here . . ."

Brendan watched him, expecting an explosion from Maura Boyd at the other end.

He was right. Even from where he was standing he could hear the shrieking and shouting down the phone line. He couldn't make out the words, but the noise sounded like a mad dog yapping. Locky held the phone away from his ear.

Then he said, "Well, thank you for being so concerned about us, Mrs Boyd, and you'll be pleased to know that we're all fine. We've had a lovely day at the Races, and we'll be coming back on the train that gets in at 7.30. I am sure you'd be happy to have a car at the station to collect us."

The yapping on the phone reached fever pitch, but Locky simply said calmly, "Thank you so much, Mrs Boyd, see you at half past seven."

He clicked the phone off and handed it back to Brendan's father, who said, "Locky, you are a real trial sometimes. Listen, I've got work to do, are you sure you'll be able to get back all right?"

"Well, we got here, didn't we?" said Locky.

"OK, but ring us when you're home." He turned to Brendan and Molly and said, "And *you* ring us when you get back to Ballygandon, do you hear?"

They promised they would, and Brendan's father went off to interview people about the Races. Molly was pleased he hadn't been there to see her parading round on La Signora. He might have gone as ballistic as Maura Boyd.

"What a wonderful day!" sighed Harriet McDonald as the train rumbled through the countryside.

"Wonderful!" her sister agreed. They all discussed their outing to the races. But Brendan thought there was an air of nervousness about the old people. They must be wondering what kind of reception they would get from the Boyds.

"We'll get off too and make sure they meet you," he told Locky.

"Better not let them see you," said his grandfather. "We don't want *you* getting into trouble as well."

They got off the train. There was no sign of

anyone there to meet them. Outside the station entrance there was a railing with a gate leading out to a small car park and the road.

"We'll wait here," said Brendan, as the three of them hid behind the railing. Locky and the others went into the car park. A few other passengers walked to the road, or got into cars and drove away.

"It looks as if they've called our bluff," said Locky. "We'll have to phone the taxi."

"I thought you were chancing it a bit, asking them to meet us," said Oliver.

Just then a Land-Rover roared into the car park and stopped suddenly. Maura Boyd got out and stormed across to Locky and his group. Brendan thought she was about to hit Locky, she looked so furious.

But instead she stood in front of him, her hands on her hips, and put her face very close to his as she snarled, "I've had just about enough of you and your goings-on, you wicked old crackpot! If you're not careful I'll have you carted off to the Funny Farm. You're not fit to be let loose!"

Locky stood his ground and simply smiled back at her. But the others hovered nearby, looking down at the ground. After she had gone on shouting for a while longer, Maura Boyd snapped, "Go on then, you gobdaws, get in!"

They clambered into the Land-Rover and Maura Boyd slammed the doors. As the Land-Rover moved away, Locky grinned from the window and gave the thumbs-up sign.

As they waited on the platform for the next train

in the Ballygandon direction, Brendan said, "I feel sorry for them going back there to Horseshoe House. Those Boyds will make life miserable for them."

"We'll really have to get our parents to tell the Boyds off," said Molly. "They'll surely take some notice of them."

But when they got back to Ballygandon, Molly found it wasn't so easy. First of all, Molly's mother had spoken to Brendan's mother in Dublin, and discovered that they had all gone to the races with Locky.

"I sometimes think your grandfather is a head-case," grumbled Molly's father.

"What did he think he was doing, bringing you all up to the Races?" said her mother. "Anything might have happened!" Molly was glad her mother didn't know exactly what had happened.

But because her parents were annoyed, they didn't take it seriously when Molly tried to tell them about the Boyds and how badly they were treating the people at Horseshoe House.

"I'm sure that's just Locky, exaggerating as usual," said Molly's father.

"But it's not only the way they treat them," said Brendan. "The Boyds are planning to cut down all the trees and build houses, and turn Horseshoe House into a health centre."

"Your imagination is too vivid for your own good, Brendan," said Molly's mother.

"But we've seen the plans!" said Dessy.

"Well, when you show us these 'plans', we'll tackle the Boyds about it."

"We haven't got them," said Brendan, "they're in the computer."

Molly's father grunted. "In the computer! A likely story!" He started reading his paper.

Later, as they played football in the yard outside the shop, Molly suddenly stopped and said, "Listen. I've just thought of something. If our parents won't believe what's going on, maybe old Mrs Boyd won't, either. When she gets our letter, she may think we're just making it all up."

"*If* she gets it," said Dessy. "If only we knew someone there who could contact her for us."

"We *do* know someone!" Molly exclaimed. "Why didn't we think of it before?"

"You're right, Molly," said Brendan excitedly. "Let's call Hollywood!"

CHAPTER NINE

The Haunting

"Hollywood?" said Dessy. "Do you mean Hollywood, California?"

"Well, I don't mean Hollywood, County Wicklow," said Brendan.

"I know what you're on about," said Molly. "You mean we contact Billy Bantam."

"Exactly," said Brendan. Billy Bantam was the boy film star they had made friends with when *The Curse of Werewolf Castle* was being filmed in Ballygandon.

"Yes, Mrs Boyd's address is in Los Angeles, and that's where Hollywood is too," said Molly. "Maybe Billy can track her down for us. We'll phone him tonight."

"Will your parents mind?" asked Brendan, remembering how they had dismissed all their complaints about Horseshoe House.

"Perhaps we won't tell them, just yet," said Molly. "If we phone in the middle of the night they won't hear us. And that will be still day-time in California. By the time they get the phone bill, they'll know what's been going on and won't mind."

At half-past twelve that night, the three of them crept downstairs. Their dog Tina got up and wagged her tail, delighted the day was starting so early. Molly patted her down. Then she dialled the number. After a few rings, she heard Billy's voice say, "Hello, Bantam residence."

"Billy, is that you? It's Molly Donovan, from Ireland."

"Hi, Molly!" Billy was delighted. "Great to hear you! How are things? How's Brendan, how's Dessy? I sure miss those fun times we had in Ballygandon."

"Yes, so do we," said Molly, keeping her voice low.

"You're very faint," said Billy. "This is a bad line."

Molly explained why she couldn't speak too loudly. Then she went on to tell Billy about their grandfather, and Horseshoe House, and the Boyds and what they were planning.

"They sound like really bad news," said Billy.

"They are," said Molly. "We need to tell Mrs Boyd as soon as we can. We hoped you could help us."

"Sure, I'll do anything I can," said Billy. Molly gave him the address. Billy said he'd try and find it and call them as soon as he had any news.

They crept up the stairs again. As they came to the window on the landing they stopped and looked out at the moonlit fields. They heard a dog howling in the distance.

"Remember when we heard those noises in the night?" said Dessy. "The creatures that sounded like werewolves?"

Molly shivered. They all remembered very well the weird things that had happened during the filming of the Werewolf movie.

"That Werewolf mask was very scary," said Dessy.

Brendan said, "Hey, that's given me an idea! Why couldn't we make a horseman look just as scary?"

"You mean the Phantom Horseman?" said Molly.

"Yes, the one that's supposed to haunt the grounds of Horseshoe House. If we can stage a visit by the Phantom Horseman, maybe we can scare the Boyds and make them stop messing with the place."

"It's worth a try," said Molly.

"Game ball," said Dessy. "When will we do it?"

"The sooner the better," said Brendan.

In the morning they had a planning session. The scheme had seemed a great idea last night, but now they could see problems. First of all, where would they find a horse? They talked about it for a long time. Could they borrow a horse from a riding school? Was there a circus anywhere near? Did one of Locky's racing friends have a spare horse?

There seemed to be no solution. Then Molly had an idea.

"The horse-drawn caravans!" she cried. "You know, the holiday caravans that people hire."

"The Phantom Horseman would look a bit stupid dragging a caravan," said Dessy.

"There'd be no caravan," said Molly. "Listen, those caravans have a set route, they start here in

Ballygandon and then go off for a week, and each night they park in a different field and untie the horses and let them loose in another field. Then they harness them up again in the morning."

"So we might be able to borrow one for the night?" asked Brendan.

"Yes, and I know just the horse! The one called Rory. I often go up to the field when he's here and feed him."

"But it's miles from here to Horseshoe House," said Brendan. "You couldn't ride him all that way and back."

"I won't have to," said Molly. "I've been working it out. The route they follow takes the caravans not far from that area, and there's a field they use behind a pub, for the horses. If they're following the usual routine, that's where they'll be tomorrow night. Now the next thing is, who's going to ride it?"

Dessy said hastily, "Well, I would do, but I twisted my ankle playing football just now . . ."

"Tell us another one, Dessy," said Brendan. "We both know that you and I would be hopeless. We'd fall off at the first gallop. No, it's got to be Molly. She's a terrific rider."

"OK, if that's what you guys think is best," Molly grinned.

Another problem was the costume. They needed something which looked spooky.

"What about sheets?" suggested Dessy.

"Fine," said Molly, "I can take two off my bed and bring them with us."

"But ghosts are meant to kind of glow in the dark, as well," said Brendan.

"How about this?" said Dessy. He produced the day-glo yellow belt and the strap he wore when he was riding his bike in the dark. The material was fluorescent and shone in the dark. They each had similar ones. They decided to cut them up and stick them to the sheets, and then put a strip of the material round Molly's head. Then Brendan and Dessy would point the beams of flash-lights from the woods at her, to make the yellow fabric glow.

"I've got some fluorescent star stickers on my ceiling," said Molly. "We could get some more of those and put them on the sheets."

"We need some sound effects too," said Dessy.

So they spent a happy half-hour making screams and howls and maniac laughter into Brendan's pocket tape-recorder, until Tina the dog set up a loud howling of her own, and Molly's father came out of the shop to shut them all up.

They told him they were rehearsing for a show they were going to put on for the old people at Horseshoe House.

"I don't know why you spend so much time at that place, if it's as awful as you claim," said Molly's father.

"We like to cheer them up," said Molly.

Her father smiled. "Well, I hope those weird noises will amuse them," he said doubtfully.

When they got to Horseshoe House Locky told them that Gemma Danaher had rung to say she would come down the next day to look at the Monument and tell the Boyds that no one was allowed to mess about with it.

They told him about their phone call to Billy

and their plans for the haunting. Locky said he and the others would somehow get the Boyds to look the right way at the right time. With any luck the fright would make them think twice about their plans for Horseshoe House.

He also said he would telephone Molly's home later on and explain that they had missed the last bus and would stay over at Horseshoe House. When the haunting was over and the Boyds had gone to bed, he would sneak them into the living room where there were sofas and armchair cushions they could sleep on.

It was just getting dark when the three of them approached the field where the horses were kept for the night. They climbed over the fence and gazed at the shadowy forms of the horses scattered across the field, quietly munching the grass. Brendan carried a rope to tie round Rory's neck and Dessy had a bag of oats and nuts to give him.

"Hey, these don't taste too bad," he said, chewing.

"Don't eat those, they're for Rory," said Molly.

"Besides, they make your teeth grow long like a horse's," said Brendan.

"Maybe I could get a part in a vampire movie," Dessy said.

"Keep quiet," said Molly. "I think I know which one is Rory. Follow me, men!" Crouching down, she moved slowly across the field towards one of the horses. The other two followed.

Molly stopped beside the horse. "Hello, Rory old fellow," said Molly, stroking his neck. The horse raised his head and looked round. "Give me the oats and nuts." Molly stretched out her hand, with the palm flat, and Dessy tipped a sprinkling of the food on it.

Molly held her hand towards Rory's mouth. He sniffed the palm of her hand with his muzzle and then began to eat. "Put the rope over him," Molly whispered. Brendan slipped the rope over Rory's head. The horse jerked his head up, but Brendan held on firmly and Molly murmured, "There, there, Rory, good boy." The horse returned to his eating.

They led Rory out of a gate that opened into another field, and then on to a pathway that led into the woods at the edge of the Horseshoe House estate.

They stopped and tied Rory to a tree. He seemed contented enough, munching the oats and nuts they put on the ground for him.

Molly took the sheets out of her rucksack and draped them round herself. They had the pieces of yellow day-glo fabric and the fluorescent stars already stuck to them. She put a white skull-mask over her face, and a white cycling helmet on her head.

"You look really scary," said Dessy. "I hope you won't frighten Rory." But the horse took no notice of the apparition, and munched on.

Brendan checked the tape recorder was working. When everything was ready, they sat down to wait. There was an hour before the time they had arranged with Locky. The minutes passed slowly.

Even Dessy couldn't think of any jokes to tell. He took a packet of sweets out of his pocket and passed them round. As he was taking one himself, a large, wet nose came over his shoulder and the bag was snatched from his hand. Rory had decided that he wanted a share.

But Dessy could only stare glumly as Rory took not just a share, but the whole bag. He munched at it greedily, paper and all.

"That horse has no manners," said Dessy.

"You can say that again!" yelled Brendan, leaping out of the way, as a stream of liquid came from the horse and splashed on to the ground. All three of them kept well away until the horse had finished.

"I suppose it's just as well he got that over with," said Molly. "Whoever heard of a peeing Phantom Horse?"

When the time came, they led Rory into the wood, till they were in sight of Horseshoe House. Then they went a roundabout way and came to the shed which Locky and Oliver had painted. They pushed open the door and led Rory inside. From here they could see the side of the house which faced towards the woods and the monument. They waited.

"It's over there! Quick! Get the fire brigade!" It was Locky's voice. He came out of the house, followed by Oliver and the McDonald sisters, and Gerry and Maura Boyd. Locky led the group into the wood, then stopped.

"I can't see any fire," they heard Gerry Boyd say.

"You're talking nonsense, as usual," said Maura.

"No, he's not, I'm sure I saw something too," said Harriet McDonald.

"You're all barmy!" said Gerry Boyd. He turned to go back to the house.

"Right!" said Brendan, "let the haunting begin!"

Molly climbed on to Rory's back and clung to the rope around his neck. She was used to riding him round the field bareback, when the caravan owners weren't looking, so he trotted amiably through the wood, with Molly murmuring encouraging words.

Brendan and Dessy crept into the woods behind her, each of them carryng a flashlight.

When they heard Locky cry out, "Look! Look over there!" Brendan started his tape-recorder and they both switched on their lights, pointing the beam towards Molly. As arranged, the McDonald sisters started shrieking and Locky and Oliver called out, "The Phantom! It's the Phantom!"

It was a really eerie sight. The beams of light picked out the luminous yellow streaks and stars on the white costume, which billowed out behind Molly as she rode along. The wails and howls and laughter from the tape echoed through the woods.

Molly rode towards the Monument. The cries from the spectators grew louder. Brenda McDonald gave an ear-piercing scream. It was so loud that it alarmed Rory. The horse reared up on his hind legs and whinnied. Somehow, Molly held on.

Coming down to earth again, Rory decided to get away from all the hubbub as quickly as he could. He began to canter through the woods towards the monument. Still Molly clung to his neck. Then she cried, "No, Rory, no! You'll never make it!"

The horse was heading straight for the monument. For a moment, Molly thought he was going to try to jump over it. But he drew up so sharply that Molly was catapulted over his neck and landed on top of the monument. She clung on to the ivy-covered roof and listened to Rory as first he pounded the ground with his hooves, then galloped off through the wood.

Brendan and Dessy switched off their flashlights and the tape-recorder and crouched down out of sight in the undergrowth.

The sudden silence was strange. An owl hooted. Molly could feel her heart pounding. She was a bit scratched, but otherwise she wasn't hurt. In the distance she heard Maura Boyd's voice saying, "Get inside! Get inside, all of you!"

She decided to stay where she was until the coast was clear. She hoped Brendan and Dessy hadn't been discovered. They too must have decided to lie low for the moment.

Molly gripped the ivy. She felt her hand touch something hard and cold, like metal.

She pushed her hand in under the ivy. The tip of something metal was poking out from a deep crack in the roof of the monument. Molly took hold of the metal tip and pulled at it. Gradually she eased out the object and untangled it from the ivy. She looked at it and her eyes widened with excitement. It was a horseshoe!

CHAPTER TEN

Proofs and Pretences

Molly peered at the horseshoe. It was old and rusty. It must be the horseshoe in the story – the one that was left there the night Daniel fell from his horse and was killed. The legend said that when the horseshoe was found, a threat of doom would be lifted from the House. And here it was! Molly hoped that now Horseshoe House would be safe and her grandfather and his friends would still have a home.

She was relieved to see the beam of a torch coming towards the monument through the woods. Brendan and Dessy must be approaching.

She was just about to call out to them, when she heard Maura Boyd's voice. "Shine that light, Gerry, I'm sure whoever it was must be still round here somewhere."

Molly lay flat and pulled some of the strands of ivy over her. In any case, she hoped the battlements round the roof would prevent anyone seeing her from the ground.

"You don't suppose it could have been . . ." Gerry's voice trailed away. He sounded nervous.

"Could have been what?" snapped Maura. "The Phantom Horseman? Don't be so stupid."

"Well, the locals do say . . ."

"The locals are a bunch of superstitious idiots!" said Maura. "It was somebody playing a trick to try and scare us. I wouldn't be surprised if that Locky is mixed up in it – and those sickening grandchildren of his."

By now the Boyds were at the Monument and circling round it, shining the torch. Molly lay flat and still, with her face down. She hoped the phosphorescent stripes wouldn't draw attention to her, but luckily the battlements round the roof hid her from view. The ivy was tickling her nose. She desperately wanted to sneeze.

"There's no sign of anyone," said Gerry Boyd, his voice shaky. "Whatever it was has vanished now. Let's pack it in and go back indoors."

"They won't get away with this," said Maura menacingly as they turned and made their way back through the woods.

Molly hoped that Brendan and Dessy were well hidden. Thank goodness Rory had gone galloping off among the trees. No doubt he had found his way back to the caravan field by now. Molly smiled. The horse had acted his part really well.

After a few minutes, she heard Brendan's voice whisper, "Molly, Molly . . . where are you? Are you OK?"

She looked over the edge of the roof. "I'm fine," she said, startling her friends below. "And I've got something to show you!"

Brendan and Dessy were amazed to see where

Molly had landed and helped her scramble down to the ground. Molly showed them the horseshoe.

"Things are looking up," said Brendan. "When Gemma Danaher comes down here tomorrow, we'll have this as proof of how old the monument is."

"You did a great job acting the Phantom Horseman," Dessy told Molly. "You almost had *me* scared."

"I think Gerry Boyd was scared too," said Molly, taking off her sheet costume. "But that wife of his is as hard as nails, we didn't fool her."

"We'll have to lie low for the night, she mustn't find us," said Brendan.

"We'll wait here till Locky lets us know the coast is clear," said Molly.

The minutes ticked by. The moon came out and shone its dappled light through the branches of the trees. It was easy to imagine that strange shapes were moving through the woods. Then suddenly all three of them looked at each other in alarm. They had all heard it: the sound like a voice wailing faintly, the name "Aoife . . . Aoife . . . Aoife . . ." Once again it seemed to be coming from inside the monument.

"It's the wind in the ivy," said Brendan, but he didn't sound at all sure.

They were relieved to hear another sound from over towards Horseshoe House. It was the hoot of an owl. That was Locky's signal to tell them they could come back.

They made their way through the woods, and found Locky standing at the open window of the living room.

"The Boyds have gone to bed," he whispered as they reached him. "You can climb in now and spend the night in here. We phoned your parents earlier to ask them if you could stay."

They scrambled in through the window. Oliver was there too, and he showed them the sofa and some armchair cushions he had laid out on the floor as beds.

"We were able to sneak these out of our rooms too," he said, showing them some rugs and blankets.

"And I've already got sheets!" said Molly, pointing at the ghost costume she was carrying.

"And this should help to keep you going," said Oliver, producing a bag of biscuits.

"You staged a wonderful show," said Locky. "Sleep well, and don't dream of Phantom Horsemen!"

When they woke it was daylight. Brendan stood up and stretched his arms. He looked out of the window. The sun was shining through the leaves of the wood and the birds were singing. It was hard to believe all the things that had happened the night before. But Molly looked at the horseshoe and knew it had all been real. They climbed out of the window. First they made their way through the woods to the caravan horses' field. There was Rory, safely back home and nibbling happily at the grass. Then they went back and hid in the shed so that the Boyds wouldn't see them.

Locky had arranged to meet Gemma Danaher at the gate of the drive. He wanted to bring her through the woods to see the monument so that they didn't have to go to the House. Locky had a shrewd idea that the Boyds would not be at all pleased to have an expert checking out the monument they wanted to pull down.

Brendan, Molly and Dessy went through the woods to the gate to wait with Locky for Gemma Danaher.

As soon as Gemma stepped out of her car, Molly showed her the horseshoe. Gemma looked at it closely and turned it round and round in her hands. She took a magnifying glass out of her pocket and stared through it.

"Yes, this looks like the real thing to me," she said. "It must be two hundred years old at least. I'll take it back to Dublin and get the museum people to examine it."

They went all round the Monument and Gemma Danaher looked at it very carefully, lifting the ivy here and there to see the stone and the marble more closely.

"How did anyone get into it?" asked Locky. "There must be an entrance."

"I expect it's all grown over by the ivy," said Gemma. "When we get the museum people to look at it, they'll find the entrance. I expect they'll want to clean up the whole monument and restore it. It could look magnificent."

"It won't, if the Boyds have their way," said Locky.

"They'll flatten it!" said Dessy.

They told her all about the plans they had seen and the conversation they had heard Maura Boyd having with the developer Mixer Murphy.

"There's no way they'll get permission to touch this monument," said Gemma.

"I somehow think they weren't planning to ask for permission," said Locky.

"I'll go and see the Boyds now," said Gemma, "and tell them all about it."

"I doubt if they'll take any notice," said Brendan.

But he was wrong. He and the others sneaked into the hallway after Locky and Gemma had gone into the office with the Boyds. The door was left ajar and they were able to hear the conversation.

"Well, we're so glad you told us about this," said Maura. "Aren't we, Gerry?"

"Oh yes indeed," Gerry agreed, sounding bewildered.

"We'd hate to damage anything of such historic importance," Maura went on. "We just had no idea it was more than an old ruin."

"It's very much more than that," said Gemma. "I believe it is one of the most remarkable monuments of its period."

"And you found the horseshoe too?"

"Yes, that could give us extra proof of the date, and so on. Besides, it shows there could be some truth in the old story about Daniel riding to the rescue."

"Rescue, yes," said Maura Boyd. "Well, you can rest assured that Horseshoe House and its heritage is safe with us."

"Good," said Gemma. "Well, I'll go back to Dublin now, and you'll be hearing from the department in due course."

"Oh do let Gerry show you something of the House and grounds before you go," said Maura. "I'll join you on the tour. I must just ring Mixer Murphy and tell him that the plans have changed and we won't be needing his bulldozer any more."

Realising they were about to come out of the office, the three listeners hid under the wide stairway that led to the upper part of the house.

They heard Gerry in the hall, with Gemma and Locky. As they went out of the front door, Locky looked back, wondering where his grandchildren were. Molly peeped out from under the stairs, and put her fingers to her lips. Locky smiled, and went out after the other two.

"Well, it looks like we saved the Monument," said Dessy.

"I'm not so sure," said Brendan. They remained hidden, crouched under the stairs, talking in quiet voices.

"Maura Boyd was a bit too agreeable, if you ask me," said Molly suspiciously.

"Hey, listen, she's talking to someone," said Brendan. The office door was still ajar. Down the hall, they could hear Maura's voice.

She was speaking on the phone, asking for someone. She sounded worried.

They couldn't hear properly, so they crept out from their hiding-place and along the hallway to listen outside the office door.

"Is that Mixer Murphy?" they heard Maura say.

"Listen, Mixer, something's come up. We've got to get on with it, or the whole plan could be banjaxed. Can you get your bulldozer in here as soon as possible? Right! I'll make sure the coast is clear. And you'll get some of the money straight away. Yes, all right – cash!"

She put down the phone. They heard her coming

towards the door and once again scurried back to their hiding-place under the stairs. They saw Maura stride along the hall and out of the front door.

"We've got to stop her," said Brendan. "We must run and catch Gemma up and tell her."

"Maura Boyd would just deny it," said Molly. "You've seen how lying and smarmy she can be."

"If only the aunt in California would show up," said Dessy.

"Surely she'd ring, if Billy has found her," said Brendan. "She'll soon put a halt to their gallop."

"We've got to get hold of Billy and see what's happening," said Molly.

"It's very late in California now," said Brendan. "The Bantams won't be best pleased to be rung up."

"I know what we can do," said Molly. "We'll send him a fax. I've got his fax number in my notebook and I saw a fax machine in the office."

"What was the horseman doing, riding on a typewriter?" asked Dessy. The others glared at him. "Fax-hunting!" he laughed.

"Shut up, Dessy, this is serious," said Brendan, as they went into the office. The fax machine was on a table beside the desk. Molly took a sheet of paper from a drawer and wrote on it in big letters:

To: Billy Bantam
From: Molly, Dessy and Brendan

Dear Billy,
Urgent you reach Mrs Boyd and ask her to stop developments here. Horseshoe House threatened. Good Luck!

"How do we send it?" asked Dessy.

"I think I can work the machine," said Brendan, "my father has one at home, to send stories in to the papers." He took the paper and fed it into a slot at the side of the machine.

"Now, Molly, you dial the number," he said and Molly pushed the buttons on the top of the machine. There was a high-pitched tone and Brendan pressed the SEND key. The paper began to be sucked in and slowly emerged from a slot at the other side. A little screen said, ONE PAGE SENT.

"Magic!" said Dessy.

"That should do the trick," said Brendan.

They heard footsteps outside the front door. "We gotta get outta here!" said Dessy urgently. They rushed to the door of the office, then Molly dashed back again and snatched the piece of paper with the message on it from the fax machine. Soon they were under the stairs again.

The front door opened. It was Locky. He looked around the hall. Brendan leaned out and waved to him.

Locky came across to them and said quietly "The Boyds are seeing Gemma off. I came back to check you were OK and plan what to do now."

They told him of their doubts about Maura Boyd's sincerity. Locky agreed. "She was just too nice to be true," he said. "But I've got a little scheme. I'll tell Maura that Oliver and I would like to do some weeding and clearing up around the monument, so it will be ready for the experts. That way we can keep an eye on it – and Maura can hardly complain since she's pretending to go along with Gemma's plan."

"Good thinking, Grandpa," said Brendan.

"Here they are now," said Locky, as the front door opened. "Keep yourselves hidden." Maura Boyd came in.

"What are you doing here?" she snapped at Locky.

"I wanted to see you, Mrs Boyd," said Locky. "I've got a plan to help you and I wanted to have a word with you about it."

"All right, all right, come into the office," said Maura Boyd, leading the way in.

The door closed. They could just hear the voices talking in the office. "Let's sneak out now," said Brendan, "we can go into the woods and meet Grandpa and Oliver at the monument."

They were just about to leave the shelter of the stairway when the office door was thrown open and Maura Boyd stormed out, clutching a piece of paper. She was swearing and cursing. She opened the front door and went out.

"Gerry! Gerry!" she shouted. "Get a look at this!" She rushed off down the drive to find her husband.

Locky peeped out of the office as the door slammed behind Maura Boyd.

"What was all that about?" asked Brendan.

"A fax came in," said Locky. "I couldn't see what it said, but I saw the top line. It said *Dear Brendan, Molly and Dessy . . .*"

"Oh NO!" cried Molly. "It must have been Billy, replying to *our* fax! Why did he send it to the office?"

"The fax always prints the number you're sending from," said Brendan. "He must have thought it was a safe number we could use. If only we knew what he said."

"Whatever it was, it seems to have sent Maura Boyd into orbit!" said Dessy.

"Well, there's only one way to find out," said Molly. "Whatever the time is in California, we'll have to ring Billy and ask him."

In the office, they dialled Billy in California.

"Hi, you guys!" said Billy. "I got your fax. I was watching an old movie in the den where the fax machine is when it came through . . . I thought I'd answer you right away. You got the good news?"

"What good news?" asked Brendan.

"The good news in my fax," said Billy. "I found Mrs Boyd and told her what was happening. She went to the airport at once. She's on her way home to surprise that pair of crooks and save Horseshoe House."

"Thanks, Billy!" said Brendan. "You're a star."

"Say, you don't sound too happy," said Billy. "Is there a problem?"

"None that we can't sort out," said Brendan. He didn't want to tell Billy that his eagerness had misfired.

"See you in California some time!" said Billy. "Don't forget, you're all invited!"

"Thanks again," said Brendan. "See you there!"

He turned to the others and said, "He found Mrs Boyd. She's on her way here now. She's going to give them a surprise."

"The only trouble is," said Molly, "it's not a surprise any more. Maura and Gerry will be expecting her. Things could get very nasty!"

CHAPTER ELEVEN

Dark Discoveries

"Things will certainly get nasty if they find us in the office here," said Locky. "We'll go to the living room and plan our campaign."

They all went out into the hall and Locky was about to close the door behind him when the telephone in the office rang. They looked at one another.

"Shall we answer it?" asked Molly.

"It might be Mixer Murphy," said Brendan. "We could maybe find something out."

"Right," said Locky, "you go on into the living room and I'll find out who it is." He went back into the office and picked up the phone, saying, "Horseshoe House."

In the living room Brendan told Oliver and the McDonald sisters what had happened.

"It will be wonderful to have Mrs Boyd back again," said Harriet.

"I hope she gets here in time, before Gerry and Maura turn us all out," said her sister.

When Locky came in, he was grinning widely.

95

"That was your mother," he told Molly. "She asked are you ever coming home, or have you taken early retirement and joined the old folks here!"

"What did you say, Grandpa?" asked Molly.

"I told them you were being a great help here at Horseshoe House."

"It's true," said Dessy. "We could advertise ourselves: *The Ballygandon Gang – Houses haunted by arrangement.*"

"Well, I didn't actually mention the haunting," said Locky, "but your mother said she was glad you were making yourselves useful."

"For once," said Molly, smiling.

"Yes, she did say 'for once' – I wasn't going to tell you that," said Locky. "Anyway, I praised you so much that she agreed you could stay on here for today and carry on helping."

"Thanks, Grandpa," said Molly.

"And you'll never guess who was there – Carrie! She had called to see you."

"Did you talk to her?" asked Molly.

"Sure. I suggested she come over here."

"The Boyds won't be too pleased to see her," said Brendan.

"That's what she thought too, so I told her to meet us down by the monument later on."

"If only Gemma hadn't gone," said Molly, "we could have told her about the fax and how angry Maura was, and what she said to Mixer Murphy. She could have brought the department people in to help us."

"I know what we can do," said Locky. "She

should be on the way to Dublin now. We'll get her to turn round and come back here."

"Well, I'm a good runner, but I don't think even I could catch up a car," said Dessy.

"She's got a car phone," said Locky. He opened the door and looked out into the hall. There was no sign of the Boyds. He went into the hall and across to the office to use the phone.

When he came back he was looking puzzled. "There was no reply from Gemma's car phone," he said. "So I telephoned her office, but she wasn't there either. They said they'd expected her to phone in, but there was no sign of her."

"Perhaps she's mitching," said Dessy.

"I keep telling you, Dessy, this is serious," said Brendan.

"Well, *I* take mitching very seriously, I often do it," said Dessy.

"I know, and from what I remember, the school takes your mitching seriously too!" said Brendan. "I sometimes wonder why you bother to turn up at all."

"So do I," said Dessy.

"This isn't getting us anywhere," said Molly. "What are we going to do about Gemma?"

"We'll just have to try again later," said Locky. "Meanwhile, let's get down to the monument. I told Maura Boyd that Oliver and I would go and weed and clean up around it. That way we'll be there if she and Gerry try anything on."

It seemed almost eerily quiet in the woods. The sky had clouded over and the only sound was the rustle of leaves in the slight wind. They began to potter about around the monument, pretending to be busy, but really keeping a look-out to see if they could see what the Boyds were up to. But there was no sign of them.

"Hello there!" Carrie's voice greeted them.

There were great welcomes and reunion hugs and then they sat on the steps of the monument and told Carrie of all that had happened and how Horseshoe House and the whole estate was in great danger.

"We hoped we could get Gemma Danaher to come back," said Molly. "She'd help to sort them out."

"Perhaps she *has* come back," said Carrie. "There was a car I didn't know, parked not far from the gate."

"What kind of car?" asked Locky.

"A Volvo, I think."

"That's what Gemma was driving," said Brendan.

"So she *has* come back!" said Dessy. "She hasn't gone mitching after all."

"If she's come back, then where is she?" asked Molly.

"That's what puzzles me," said Locky.

"Perhaps she didn't come back," said Oliver. "Perhaps she never left at all."

They looked at one another in alarm. The explanation seemed very likely and, if it was true, then what could have happend to Gemma?

"The last I saw of her," said Locky, "was when I

was walking down the drive with her and Gerry Boyd, to go to her car. I said goodbye to her and came back to the House to see all of you. Gerry was being very nice to her. I assumed she'd got into the car and driven off to Dublin."

"Perhaps the car wouldn't start," said Oliver.

"She'd have come back to the House in that case," said Locky.

"Maybe the Boyds tricked her," said Molly. "What if they fixed the car so it wouldn't start, then Gerry said he'd drive her to the station, then took her off into the country and left her?"

"Or perhaps he brought her back to the House and they locked her up somewhere," said Dessy.

"Could be," said Locky. "I'll go to the House and hunt around."

But as he was about to set off they saw two figures approaching through the wood. Harriet and Brenda McDonald were stumbling and crashing through the undergrowth towards them, waving their arms in the air.

"They're here, they're here!" cried Brenda.

"We must stop them, we must stop them!" puffed Harriet.

"Keep calm," said Oliver, who didn't sound very calm himself.

"Who's here? Who must we stop?" asked Locky.

"The bulldozer!" said Harriet. "We saw it from the back of the House, coming up through the woods. It stopped by the house and the driver got off and the Boyds came out and talked to him."

"Was he wearing a tweed cap?" asked Molly.

"That's right, he was," said Brenda.

"That must have been Mixer Murphy, the developer the Boyds were plotting with," said Brendan.

"Well, whoever he was," said Harriet, "he started the bulldozer again and headed into the woods in this direction. So we came out to warn you."

Then, in the distance, they heard the throb of an engine.

"There it is!" said Dessy. "Over there, in the trees!" They looked into the woods. Among the trees they could see the bright yellow colour of the big bulldozer with its front scoop going up and down as it crashed its way through the undergrowth.

"It's coming this way," shrieked Brenda McDonald. "It will flatten us all!"

"We'll stop him!" said Brendan.

"How?" asked Harriet fearfully.

"We'll stage a protest, like those people who want to stop motorways being built," Brendan declared.

"Yeah," said Dessy. "We'll build some tree-houses and live in them so they can't chop the trees down."

The McDonald sisters looked at him in dismay.

"We haven't time to do that, Dessy," said Brendan. "We'll lie down in front of the bulldozer. That's what those protesters do."

He and Molly set off through the wood towards the bulldozer. Carrie and Dessy followed close behind. Then came Locky and Oliver and at the back the McDonald sisters, doing their best to pick their way through the undergrowth without getting tangled up in it.

When Brendan and Molly got near the bulldozer, they took a stand right in its path. Carrie and Dessy drew up beside them. They stood in a line like footballers facing a penalty shot.

The bulldozer stopped. Mixer Murphy leaned out of the cab and shouted, "Get out of the way!"

No one moved. "I said clear off!" said Mixer Murphy. "What's the matter, are you deaf or something?"

By this time, Locky, Oliver and the McDonald sisters had joined the line. They stared defiantly at Mixer Murphy.

"For the last time, clear off, or you'll get hurt!" he said. Then, when no one moved, he growled, "OK, but don't say I didn't warn you!" He moved the controls and a great roar came from the bulldozer as it revved up. At the same time, the scoop rose high in the air.

Harriet McDonald shrieked. Her sister began to sob.

"Don't worry," said Locky. "You two go back and keep an eye on the monument. We'll be all right, I'm sure he's bluffing." But Locky didn't sound all that sure and as he spoke the bulldozer gave another roar. The McDonalds scurried away, stumbling back to the monument.

"Right, this is it!" said Locky. He lay down on the ground, and all the others did the same. They could hear Mixer Murphy cursing. The machine gave another roar and the giant scoop moved downwards towards them. Then it paused in mid-air, and the engine stopped.

Mixer Murphy got down from the cab and strode across to them. "I don't know what you think you're playing at," he said, "but I've got a job to do and I mean to do it. So if you won't move, I'll go and get someone to move you!"

He marched off through the woods towards the House. They all laughed with relief.

"Victory!" said Brendan.

"For the time being," said Locky. "I'm sure he'll be back with some of his men, and the Boyds too. It will be hard for us to resist strong-arm tactics."

They all stood up. They heard Harriet McDonald over beside the monument, calling out, "Help! Help!"

They went through the woods towards her. Both the sisters were calling and beckoning to them.

When they reached them, Harriet said, "We heard a noise, a kind of faint wail, like a voice."

"It came from inside there," said Brenda, pointing at the monument.

Brendan and Molly looked at each other, remembering the strange lamenting cry that had seemed to come from within the monument. They all listened. Brendan and Molly put their ears against the ivy-covered stone.

Sure enough, they could hear a wailing sound, but this time it sounded more urgent and frightened, like a long-drawn out cry for help. There was a pause, then it was repeated.

"Is it a ghost?" whimpered Brenda.

"I think it's a real person," said Locky. "And I've an idea who it could be."

"Gemma?" asked Molly.

"Exactly," said Locky. "Gerry Boyd must have brought her here and locked her up so that she couldn't do anything to put a stop to their plans."

"We must find the entrance," said Brendan.

"But we've looked at every inch of the walls," said Molly, "and we couldn't find anything."

"When I was running back here just now," said Harriet McDonald, "I nearly tripped on something hard, like iron. It was a sort of metal ring. I thought it must be some junk someone had left."

"It sounds like the handle of a trap-door," said Molly.

"Where was it?" asked Brendan.

"Just over here, I think." Brendan and Molly followed her.

She pointed at the ground, and they knelt down and began brushing away the dead leaves and bits of bracken.

"Look there!" said Molly. They could see an old rusty circle of iron, lying on the ground.

"It's attached to a sort of bolt," said Brendan. The others gathered round and they all scraped away at the ground.

"It *is* a trap-door!" Dessy exclaimed. "That iron ring must be for pulling it up."

He and Brendan grabbed hold of the ring and heaved. Slowly, a hinged slab in the ground opened. There were stone stairs leading down.

Brendan took out his pocket torch and started down the stairs, followed by Molly and Dessy, while the others kept watch outside.

Now they could hear the voice quite clearly, coming from down a stone passage-way. "Help! Help! Is anyone there?"

It was Gemma Danaher. They hurried along the passage and found some more steps at the far end. They climbed them and came up into a big stone chamber. It was damp and cold. Brendan shone his torch, and it gleamed on some white bones strewn on the stone floor. Then in the far corner, it lit up the figure of Gemma.

She was sitting against a wall, with her arms wrapped round herself, shivering.

"Thank God you found me!" she said. "I was beginning to think I'd be here for ever."

They led her back down the passage-way, up the stairs and out through the trap-door. They all greeted her and Locky gave her a great hug.

Oliver took off his coat and put it round Gemma. They sat down on the steps of the Monument. She told them that when Locky left her with Gerry going down the drive towards her car, Gerry said he had suddenly remembered something he had seen at the monument – something that could be a vital clue for the experts. He said he would like her to see it. So they went away from the drive and into the woods, till they came to the monument.

"Gerry pushed the leaves away," said Gemma, "then he grabbed the iron ring and lifted the trap-door. He said he would hold it up while I took a look inside. But as soon as I went down the stairs, he let the trap-door fall shut."

"What did you do?" asked Locky.

"I shouted and pushed at it but it was too heavy to move. I was trapped. Then a very strange thing happened. I heard Gerry give a loud scream, as though he was really frightened. Then he cried out, 'NO! NO!' and screamed again. Then he seemed to stumble away."

"What scared him, I wonder?" asked Molly.

"A horse, I think. After he'd let down the trap-door, I heard the thudding of horses' hooves. They seemed to come right up to the trap-door, then stop for a moment or two. Then they started again, over on the far side of the Monument, and disappeared. Yet, when we came through the wood, there was certainly no sign of any horses."

Everyone was silent. Molly and Brendan looked at each other.

They both thought they knew what Gerry had seen and Gemma had heard: The Phantom Horseman. And this time he had succeeded in jumping over the monument!

CHAPTER TWELVE

Race Against Time

"I think this means the threat to the House has been lifted," said Brendan.

"I'm not so sure," said Dessy. "There's trouble on the way." He pointed over towards the House. They could see Mixer Murphy striding through the woods with Maura and Gerry Boyd.

"I'd better make myself scarce," said Carrie. "I'll hide behind the monument."

"I'll do the same, for the moment," said Gemma. "It's best if they think I'm still shut up in the monument."

They went round behind the monument as Mixer Murphy and the Boyds approached. Maura seemed to be almost dragging Gerry along.

"Why didn't you tell me that's where you shut her up?" said Maura. "We might have bulldozed her too."

"She's probably died of fright by now anyway," Gerry wailed. "I'm not going near that place, it's haunted. That horse nearly ran me down!"

"Shut up, you're babbling again!" snapped

Maura. She turned to Mixer and asked, "Now, Mixer, what's all this about?"

"There they are!" said Mixer. "That bunch of kids and old fogeys. They lay down in front of my bulldozer. How can I start levelling your land if they're going to do that? You should keep better control of your residents."

"And you should keep better control of your tongue!" Maura retorted. "Otherwise you won't get your hands on any of that cash. So we'll just get that interfering woman out of there, and then you can get on with it and flatten this monument, and don't let yourself be scared by this bunch of rabble."

"I'm not scared of anyone," said Mixer Murphy, marching across towards his bulldozer.

"Pull up the trap-door and and go in and get her out, Gerry," Maura ordered. "There's nothing she can do now. She can't save a monument that's already flattened to the ground."

Gerry was quivering with fear as he looked at the trap-door. "No, Maura, please!" he whimpered. "Don't make me go in there!"

"It's all right, you won't need to," said Gemma, stepping out from behind the Monument.

"It's another ghost!" Gerry screamed. "That wretched woman went and died in there and now she's come back to haunt me!"

"Oh, I'll haunt you, don't you worry!" Gemma moved towards him and he backed away fearfully.

"Get away, get away, don't touch me!" he cried, flailing his arms in the air.

"Shut up, you idiot!" said Maura. "She's real enough. You couldn't even keep her locked up properly."

"Yes, I'm real," said Gemma sternly, "and you'll find the Guards are real too, when I ring them and get them over here."

"And where will you ring from?" Maura sneered. "You're on my property and you're not leaving. And you're certainly not using my telephone!"

"As you wish," said Gemma. "Carrie, would you run down to the gate and use my car phone to get the Guards?"

"Of course," said Carrie, coming out from her hiding-place. "I'd be delighted."

"Carrie! What are you doing here? I sacked you!" said Maura Boyd.

"It's all right, I was just leaving," said Carrie, and she ran off through the woods towards the gate.

"Here, what's all this about the Guards?" said Mixer Murphy. "I don't want anything to do with *them*."

"Then you'd better be off," said Gemma. "They'll be here soon to investigate a few things like kidnapping, fraud, destruction of ancient monuments, forging documents, getting money by false pretences . . ."

"Well, they're not investigating *me*, that's for sure!" said Mixer Murphy. He turned to Maura Boyd and said, "You can keep your fancy schemes and your luxury housing plans. I'm getting out of here before the whole thing blows up in your faces. I should have known it was too good to be true."

He climbed into the cab of the bulldozer and it roared into life. He turned it round hastily, bumping into trees and nearly pitching himself off the driver's seat. Then he crashed and rumbled off through the woods the way he had come.

Maura shouted at her husband, "This is all your fault! We'd have got away with it if it hadn't been for your bungling. You're a blithering nincompoop, that's what you are!"

"And if you hadn't been so greedy," said Gerry, "we could have cleaned up a nice little pile from these old codgers and decamped with Aunt Laura's valuables. But no, you had to start levelling the whole place and dreaming up luxury villas . . ."

"You've no vision, that's your problem, Gerry Boyd. You're a plodder!"

"And you're a grasping Gorgon!"

The others were watching this argument with interest, looking from Maura to Gerry and then back again, like spectators at a tennis match.

Then Maura turned to them and said coolly, "I'm afraid this is very undignified. You may be a bunch of fools and busybodies, but thanks to these interfering kids, you seem to have put us in the wrong. There's nothing we can do but face the music."

Gerry tried to object. "But Maura, you're not going to just give in?"

"There comes a time, Gerry," said Maura, "when you don't have any choice. Come along. We'll go and wait in the House until the Guards arrive."

She turned and began to walk slowly through

the woods in the direction of Horseshoe House. Gerry looked around him, bewildered, then hurried off and caught up with his wife. The rest watched them, getting ready to follow.

When the Boyds were a hundred metres or so ahead of them, they heard Maura turn to Gerry and say sharply, "OK, run for it!"

With surprising speed she began to sprint through the woods towards the house, with Gerry panting after her.

"Let's get after them!" said Brendan, as they set off in pursuit. But the Boyds had too much of a start. By the time Brendan, Molly and Dessy reached the front door, it slammed in their faces, and they heard the bolts being slammed shut to bar it.

"Quick, we'll go round the back!" said Dessy. But when they got to the back door, they found that was bolted too.

"At least they can't get away without us seeing them," said Brendan. "We have the house surrounded."

"But you heard what she said," Molly looked worried. "She talked about cleaning up and getting away with all the valuables. And she must have had a lot of cash ready to give to Mixer Murphy."

"What does it matter what they take if they can't get out?" said Brendan. "They'll be caught red-handed with all the stuff."

"I'd still rather know what they're up to in there," said Locky, coming up to them.

"I'll get in and open up the door," said Dessy.

"How?" asked Oliver.

Dessy pointed. "See that small window up there? It's a little bit ajar. Hoist me on your shoulders and I'll be able to reach it, and get it open and climb in."

"Be careful, Dessy," said Oliver. "They could take you hostage."

"I'll be very quiet," said Dessy as he put his foot in Brendan's cupped hands and clambered on to his shoulders, putting his hands on the wall to steady himself. Then he put his fingers into the crack and pulled. They all looked up anxiously.

"It's too stiff," Dessy called down. "I need something to prise it open."

"What about this?" said Gemma Danaher, producing the horseshoe from her bag. She reached up and handed it to Dessy.

Dessy stuck one end of the horseshoe into the crack. Then he twisted the other end and the window began to open. He pulled harder and the window opened wider.

Dessy grasped the sill and hauled himself inside. He leaned out of the window and gave the thumbs up sign to the people below.

Brendan picked up the horseshoe which had fallen to the ground. "This horseshoe is certainly bringing us luck," he grinned, handing it to Gemma Danaher.

She put it in her bag, saying, "Yes, it's helped us to save the Monument and the House. Now let's hope we can save the contents before the Boyds do a flit with them."

They went round to the front door and heard the bolts inside slide back.

"Open Sesame!" said Dessy, pulling the door open. Just then Carrie came up the drive and joined them.

"The Guards are on their way," she said.

"We must make sure the Boyds don't skedaddle before the Guards arrive," said Locky. "Harriet, would you stay here and watch the front door, while Brenda goes and watches the back? If they come out, shout and we'll all come out and grab them."

The McDonald sisters went to their posts and the others went inside.

Locky whispered, "We'll split up and go through the house in pairs. Anyone who finds the Boyds, give a great shout and try to lock them in the room. Then we'll all come and help."

Locky and Oliver made for the office. The others were going to search the upstairs rooms. Just as they were starting up the stairs they heard Locky at the door of the office call out, "Hey, look at this!"

They all crowded round the open door. Inside there was a scene of total chaos. The drawers had been pulled out of the desk and emptied, the computer was on the floor, the telephone line had been wrenched from its socket. And in the wall where a picture had been hanging was a safe. The metal door was open and there was nothing inside.

"Well, it looks as if they've taken whatever money they had," said Carrie.

"And it must have been quite a bit, considering the fees they were charging us," said Oliver.

"Not to mention the money from all the ornaments and pictures and stuff they sold off," said Locky. "We've got to hunt those robbers down."

"On with the search!" said Brendan.

"The Ballygandon Gang to the rescue!" said Molly.

They both went rushing up the stairway, followed by Carrie and Dessy. At the top of the stairs there was a suit of armour on a wooden stand.

"Hi there, Mister Tinny!" said Dessy.

"You go that way, and we'll go this," said Brendan. He and Molly went down a panelled corridor, looking in at the doors of the rooms. Some of them had been made into bed-sitting rooms for the residents and didn't seem to have been disturbed.

Then they came to a big door with an ornate brass handle. On it was a board saying in old-style black letters: PRIVATE. Molly put her fingers to her lips. They listened. From inside they could hear muttering and some scrabbling sounds.

Molly took hold of the door handle and turned it slowly. They opened the door a little way and peered inside. The room was a large bedroom with a thick floral carpet and heavy wooden furniture. Just inside the door, jutting out into the room, there was a four-poster bed with thick wooden pillars at each corner holding up a canopy. The bed was covered with a heavy tapestry coverlet with a red and gold pattern.

There were big leather chairs and a carved

113

dressing table. In front of the window there was a big oak chest. The lid was open and in front of it, with his back to them, knelt Gerry Boyd. He was hunting for something among the clothes and curtains that were stored in the chest.

"It must be here, it must be here!" he muttered, as he flung things out of the chest and rummaged inside it.

Molly looked at Brendan and pointed to the floor near the bed. Brendan nodded. They both knelt down and crawled into the space underneath the bed. The coverlet hung down all round the bed and hid them. They crawled to the end and lifted it a little so that they could see Gerry kneeling at the chest.

They saw him stop rummaging and reach in. Then he cried, "There it is!" and held up a golden bowl studded with jewels. "I knew Maura had hidden it away somewhere she thought I wouldn't find it!" he exclaimed. "Well, now it's mine. And when I get out of here, it will be my ticket to freedom. Freedom from Horseshoe House and Aunt Laura and the lot of them. And best of all, from Maura!"

As Gerry laughed and started to kiss the golden bowl in glee, Molly and Brendan smiled at each other.

"Time for a little more haunting?" whispered Molly. Brendan nodded. Molly took her tin whistle from her pocket and lying there under the bed, began to play strange, eerie sounds very softly.

They heard Gerry say in a scared voice, "What

was that? Who's there?" Brendán made some soft moaning sounds and tugged slightly at the coverlet so that it twitched a little. Then he crawled to the head of the bed and pushed his hand up under the pillows. He began slowly to pull them about.

The plan worked. Gerry said, "Stop, stop! Come out! Who's in the bed?"

Brendan gave a faint, groaning sigh. Gerry shrieked and cried, "Get away, get away! Stop haunting me!"

Then Brendan made a rhythmic tapping sound on the hollow pillar at the back of the bed which sounded like horses' hooves. Then he made a whinnying noise.

"The Horseman!" screamed Gerry, rushing to the door, clutching the golden bowl. He flung the door open and ran out into the corridor. Brendan and Molly scrambled out from under the bed and saw him stumble away down the corridor. In the distance, coming out of another corridor, they saw Dessy.

Seeing Gerry approaching, and Brendan and Molly following, Dessy darted behind the suit of armour on the landing. As Gerry reached him, the heavy arm of the knight's suit suddenly lifted up, barring his way.

From behind the armour came Dessy's voice, growling, "Not so fast, buster!"

Gerry gave a cry of fear and stumbled into the armour, which wobbled creakily, then toppled over and crashed to the floor, with Gerry tangled up in it. Dessy and Carrie sat down on top of the spreadeagled armour, pinning Gerry to the floor.

CHAPTER THIRTEEN

Caught!

A panel behind where the armour had stood slid open and the angry face of Maura Boyd looked out.

"You fool!" she shouted at Gerry. "You've given us away."

She stepped out from the secret hiding-place. She was carrying a large black brief-case. Then she snarled at Dessy and Carrie, "You meddling messers!"

Gerry said fearfully, "The Horseman, Maura, the Phantom Horseman! In the bedroom!"

"You're barmy!" said Maura. Then picking up the bowl she snapped, "You've blown it now, flashing this around. I thought I told you to put it in a pillow-case and bring it to me, so we could hide and get out through the secret stairs."

"I was going to do that, Maura, but . . ."

"He wasn't going to do that at all," said Brendan.

"No," said Molly, "he was planning to sell it for himself, and leave you."

"WHAT?" shouted Maura in disbelief.

"It's not true, Maura!" Gerry whimpered.

"You'd never leave me, you wouldn't have the guts!" said Maura.

The noise and clatter and shouts had brought Locky and Oliver up the stairs. The McDonald sisters were following them.

"Well done, the Ballygandon Gang!" said Locky, looking at the scene.

"Shut up, you doddery old bat," said Maura. "Don't think you've won yet." Then she stared at the prone form of Gerry and said, "No, you won't leave me, Gerry. But I'm going to leave *you!*"

She turned and dashed through the secret doorway, into the darkness behind. They heard the clang of her heels on metal stairs. Brendan rushed in after her, with Molly and Dessy close behind and Gemma following them.

"We'll guard the doors!" said Locky, heading down the stairs with Oliver and Carrie.

"And we'll guard *him!*" said Harriet McDonald.

"Come along, young man," said Brenda McDonald, as Gerry miserably scrambled to his feet from under the heap of armour.

Harriet picked up a metal arm which had come away from the suit, and brandished it in the air. Brenda picked up the helmet and held it in both hands, as if ready to bang it on the head of Gerry if he tried anything.

Brendan shone his torch. They could see an iron spiral staircase going down into the darkness. Maura Boyd was nearly at the bottom of it. They pounded down after her.

At the bottom, she rushed along a narrow corridor which twisted and turned. At the end of it was a small doorway. Maura Boyd ducked through it and slammed the door shut behind her. They pushed but couldn't open it. From inside they heard a metallic clatter like a big door being opened. Then there was the sound of an engine starting.

"The garage!" Brendan cried. "That's where the secret passage led. This is how they planned to get away."

"We must get in and stop her," said Molly.

"The door won't budge, we need something to bash it with," said Dessy.

"How about this?" said Gemma, producing the horseshoe from her bag. Dessy took it from her and slammed it at the door-handle.

There was a crack and the lock broke. The door flew open. They saw the Land-Rover, with Maura Boyd at the wheel, revving it up. In front of it, the garage door was open.

"Quick!" said Molly. She wrenched open the back door of the Land-Rover and scrambled in, followed by Brendan and Dessy. They crouched in the back as Maura Boyd pressed the accelerator and the Land-Rover shot forward.

It picked up speed and rocked from side to side as Maura Boyd headed around the house and into the driveway. Then they saw ahead of them, coming up the drive, the flashing blue light of a Garda car.

"Out of my way! Out of my way!" screeched

Maura, without slackening her speed. The Garda car had stopped and two Guards got out. One shouted "Stop!" and held up his hand. Maura Boyd just kept on going towards them.

"She'll flatten them!" said Dessy. "Grab the wheel!"

As Brendan and Molly grabbed Maura Boyd from the back, Dessy launched himself forward over the back seat and took hold of the steering wheel. He pulled it sharply to the left. The Land-Rover swerved crazily off the drive and into the big bushes at the side. It ploughed through one bush and into another, jolting all of them about. Finally it stalled, the engine cut out with a choke, and the vehicle stopped.

They were only a few metres away from where the Guards were standing beside their car.

"Are you OK?" Molly asked the others.

"Fine," said Brendan and Dessy together.

"Fine!" snarled Maura Boyd. "I'm sure you're fine, you horrible snotty-nosed, interfering little toads!"

"That's no way to describe the Ballygandon Gang," said Molly as they bundled Maura Boyd out of the Land-Rover. From behind her the brief-case slipped out and fell to the ground. It broke open and out of it spilled a heap of jewellery and silver, and bundles and bundles of bank-notes.

"I believe that belongs to me," said a voice nearby. Standing there was a tall woman with neat grey hair, elegantly dressed and wearing a dark blue coat.

"Laura!" Maura said angrily. "These wretched kids told you!"

"That's right," said Laura Boyd. "And it looks as if they were just in time. If it hadn't been for them, Horseshoe House would have been finished, and those elderly people turned out. As it is, their future is safe. I'm staying here to look after things, and now my daughter and her family are OK again, I know they'd like to come back and help me."

"This way – into the car," said a Guard, leading Maura Boyd away.

"Have you got room for another one in the car?" asked Molly, pointing up the driveway towards the House. A strange procession was approaching. At the head marched Locky, with Carrie beside him. Behind them shuffled Gerry Boyd, his head bowed. The McDonald sisters marched one on each side of him, brandishing their weapons from the suit of armour, and behind came Oliver, calling, "Left, right, left, right, left . . ."

They stopped when they reached the cars. Laura Boyd looked sadly at Gerry, and shook her head. "I wouldn't have believed it of you, Gerry," she said. "How could you do it?"

"I'm sorry, Aunt Laura, I'm sorry," Gerry sobbed as he got into the squad car.

When the Garda car had driven away Laura Boyd said, "We'll have a big celebration this evening. Horseshoe House and everyone living in it is safe now, thanks to all of you here."

As they all sat round the long table in the dining-room that evening, Molly and Brendan excitedly described all their adventures to their parents who had come to Horseshoe House for the celebrations.

"And then Molly dressed up in this phantom outfit . . ."

"And Brendan and Dessy shone the flashlights . . ."

"And the Phantom went galloping through the woods . . ."

Dessy and Locky and everyone else joined in with their own descriptions of the strange and hectic happenings at Horseshoe House.

"Well," said Brendan's father, "people in Dublin sometimes say the country is dull, but there's certainly been a lot of action round here."

"Game ball," said Dessy. "By the way, do you know what gave Dracula away when he tried to creep into the crypt?"

"I don't, Dessy," said Brendan, "but you're going to tell us."

"He had a fit of COFFIN!" said Dessy.

Some people groaned, others chuckled. Locky said, "Dessy's quite the comic, we're thinking of doing a double act together."

"You could call it THE DEMONIC DUO," said Molly.

"I can't wait to see that," said her father.

There was a shrill sound from the sideboard. Laura Boyd reached over and picked up a mobile phone.

"I think I know who this is," she said. "I rang him in California and asked him to call us this evening." She clicked the phone on and listened, then said, "Yes Billy, it's me, Laura Boyd. I'm back at Horseshoe House and everything is fine. I just wanted to thank you for all your help and I thought you'd like to have a word with your friends here."

She passed the phone to Molly who said, "Hi there, Billy!"

"Hi, Molly, how are you doing?" said Billy. "So you've been having great adventures over there? I wish I could have been there with the Ballygandon Gang."

"You did great for us, Billy, thanks a lot," said Molly. "And it would be terrific if you came to see us again."

"Sure I will, but before that remember you're all invited over here to Hollywood."

"Oh we'll be there, as soon as we can fix it up," said Molly, glancing at her mother and father and wondering how they could be persuaded to let her go off to California. They had never been further than Spain for a holiday, and even then her father said he didn't think they made chips like the ones back home.

Brendan and Dessy had a word with Billy too, and then Laura Boyd talked to him again. She ended by saying, "Well, I'll certainly be coming back some time to see friends there, so why don't I bring them with me, to thank them for all they've done?"

Brendan, Molly and Dessy looked at each other excitedly. Maybe a trip to Hollywood might not be such a far-fetched idea after all? Brendan thought they'd never believe it, at school.

Any more than they'd find it easy to believe all that had happened to them in these summer holidays. But he looked forward to the tales he and Dessy would be able to tell their friends when they got back.

Then he heard Locky saying, "I'd like to propose a toast and a vote of thanks, to my two brave grandchildren and their friend Dessy, for saving our home here, Mrs Boyd's Horseshoe House."

"Hear, hear!" said the McDonald sisters together. Everyone raised their glasses and said, "To Brendan, Molly and Dessy!"

"Thanks," said Molly and Brendan, while Dessy stood up and took a bow.

Brendan raised his own glass and said, "I'd like to give a toast to Daniel and Aoife. Perhaps they're together now in spirit, and he won't still be crying her name from the Monument. So here's to the Phantom Horseman!"

The McDonald sisters again said "Hear, hear!" and glasses were raised once more.

"A pity he couldn't trot along and join us," said Dessy. Then he looked puzzled. Could that sound they seemed to hear, from over there in the woods, possibly be the triumphant thud of horses' hooves . . . ?